"We must consult Venus to learn the identity of your soul mate."

"Soul mate?" Lord Dearborn echoed incredulously.

Madame Fortunata took no notice. "I have all the details now. You are certain to marry within the year. She is tall for a woman and sculpted like the goddess herself. Hair of gold and eyes as blue as the sky. A vision of loveliness, soon to come to London for the first time. I can tell you no more."

Madame Fortunata's words came back to him not long afterward when he escorted his mother to a musicale at Lady Seabrook's. His glance took in various newcomers to the social scene. The family just entering the room held him spellbound. Two daughters, one small and dark, not in his style at all, and the other . . . tall, golden haired, lovely. As the group moved into the room, he was struck by the grace of her stride.

His head in a whirl at this sudden materialization of his fanciful daydream, Lord Dearborn approached to seek an introduction to the woman who was clearly his destiny. . . .

Regency England: 1811-1820

"It was the best of times, it was the worst of times...."

As George III languished in madness, the pampered and profligate Prince of Wales led the land in revelry and the elegant Beau Brummel set the style. Across the Channel, Napoleon continued to plot against the English until his final exile to St. Helena. Across the Atlantic, America renewed hostilities with an old adversary, declaring war on Britain in 1812. At home, Society glittered, love matches abounded and poets such as Lord Byron flourished. It was a time of heroes and villains, a time of unrelenting charm and gaiety, when entire fortunes were won or lost on a turn of the dice and reputation was all. A dazzling period that left its mark on two continents and whose very name became a byword for elegance and romance.

Books by Brenda Hiatt

HARLEQUIN REGENCY ROMANCE
70—GABRIELLA
81—THE UGLY DUCKLING

LORD DEARBORN'S DESTINY

BRENDA HIATT

Harlequin Books

TORONTO • NEW YORK • LONDON
AMSTERDAM • PARIS • SYDNEY • HAMBURG
STOCKHOLM • ATHENS • TOKYO • MILAN
MADRID • WARSAW • BUDAPEST • AUCKLAND

For Betty Barber, Riley Morse and Julie Caille,
with heartfelt thanks

Published February 1993

ISBN 0-373-31191-5

LORD DEARBORN'S DESTINY

CHAPTER ONE

"WON'T YOU AT LEAST consider it, Forrest? As a favour to me?" The Countess of Dearborn cocked her head at her son in a manner intended to be winsome, but which made her enormous purple turban tip dangerously to one side.

"Don't tell me you would actually believe anything this Madame Fortunata might say, Mother," he replied with a snort, one golden brow sceptically arched. "I can assure you that I won't."

"Then you'll come?" Lady Dearborn was ecstatic. "I promise you won't regret it. Fortunata isn't Cora's real name, of course; I knew her when she was plain Mrs. Lawrence, back when she did readings only for a few friends, but now she is become ever so popular. Having one's fortune told is all the thing these days, you know."

"So is pink embroidery on one's waistcoat, I have heard, but you'll notice that my own singularly lacks it."

"Now, Forrest, don't tease," said the countess, rising with a flutter of feathers and scarves to lay a tiny beringed hand on her son's sleeve. "You know how much this means to me."

He did. For as long as Forrest could remember, Lady Dearborn had relied heavily on superstition, folk tales and charms to order her daily life. As a child, he had been forced to eat gooseberries, which he detested, every Whit Sunday as well as pancakes, which he liked rather better, on Shrove Tuesday. And he could still vividly recall, at a distance of some twenty years, his mother's hysteria over a maid's broken looking-glass, presaging ill luck for the entire household. The fact that her worst fears were never realized had no apparent effect on her blind faith in such omens.

"I will come, Mother. But I warn you—" his deep blue eyes narrowed "—do not expect me to do anything foolish, no matter how many offspring your Gypsy foretells for me. *If* I marry, 'twill be to someone of my own choosing and in my own time."

"Certainly, Forrest, certainly!" agreed Lady Dearborn in shocked accents. "I would never presume to make such a decision for you."

The Earl of Dearborn smiled in spite of himself. "No, only to nudge me in the proper direction. Do you really want grandchildren so desperately as all that?"

"I'll not say another word on the subject," declared the countess, her chin in the air. "Cora's predictions must speak for themselves." She rang for her abigail, a middle-aged woman as stolid and sensible as her mistress was flamboyant and eccentric. "My amethyst cloak, Marie, and the lilac-and-silver scarf."

Marie extracted the required items from a wardrobe overflowing with feathers, scarves and gauzes of every hue, with shades of purple and red predominating. A sleek Siamese cat batted at the scarf as it wafted past, but Marie, with deftness born of long practice, whisked it up out of reach of the playful sable paw.

Well wrapped against the early April chill, Lady Dearborn paused long enough to tuck a curled silver feather into her turban. Nodding at her reflection in the dressing-table mirror, she turned to her son and pronounced herself ready to leave.

"I trust Madame Fortunata will not be long-winded with her prognostications," observed the earl as they descended to his waiting curricle. "I am expected for nuncheon at White's before one."

FOLLOWING HIS mother's directions, Lord Dearborn was surprised when she told him to rein in his pair before a perfectly respectable-looking Town house of ample proportions on Brook Street.

"Your Madame Fortunata lives here?" he asked incredulously. "She must do exceedingly well gulling the ton out of their money."

"Cora is only Madame Fortunata on Tuesday and Thursday mornings," the countess explained. "The rest of the time she is Mrs. Lawrence, as I said before, and quite well received. I daresay you have met her at some of the dos yourself."

"Indeed" was the earl's only comment. Leaving his groom to walk the horses to prevent their becoming chilled, he escorted his mother up the broad front stairs where a butler, looking much like any other butler in London, admitted them to the house.

"Sylvia, my dear!" Rising to meet them as they entered a parlour that was in no way out of the ordinary

was a short, matronly woman, dressed far more con-
servatively than the countess. "You induced him to
come, I see." Turning to the earl, she said cryptically,
"Your mother has warned me that you are a sceptic,
my lord, so I thought it best that we meet first in
here."

"I am charmed to make your acquaintance, Mrs.
Lawrence—or is it Madame Fortunata today? It is
Thursday, is it not?"

Their hostess gave a long, tinkling laugh. "A sceptic indeed, I see! It is only in my astrological sanctum
that I become Madame Fortunata, my lord, while in
any other part of the house I remain plain Cora
Lawrence." She waved him to a chair, seating herself
across from him. "Will you have a cup of tea, or
would you prefer that we begin forthwith?" Her
question was directed at the earl, but she glanced at
Lady Dearborn for guidance as she spoke.

"Forrest did say something about another engagement . . ." she began.

"Yes, yes, let us get the mumbo jumbo over with,"
said the earl quickly. "I've no doubt my mother has
told you to predict eight or ten brats for me over the
next dozen years. Not that I intend to comply." He
glanced sidelong at the countess, who feigned great
interest in the gilded moulding of the mantelpiece.
"Where is this astrology room of yours?"

Mrs. Lawrence appeared more amused than of-
fended at his manner. "Very well, my lord, I see we
must waste as little of your precious time as possible.
This way, if you please." Rising smoothly, she led the

way out of the parlour and across the front hall to a door at the base of the curving staircase.

Watching Mrs. Lawrence walking ahead of them in her fashionable pearl-grey, high-necked morning gown, Forrest found it difficult to reconcile her unremarkable appearance with his mother's stories of her uncanny ability as a fortune-teller. Cora Lawrence looked like any of a dozen other Society matrons he had met at various respectable gatherings.

"Wait here a moment," she said before disappearing behind the plain, oak-panelled door. No more than a minute later, she called out from within, "You may enter now."

Without hesitation, the earl turned the knob and pushed open the door, only to stand mesmerized on the threshold. The room, apparently windowless, was lit by a single candle on a small table at its centre. Cloth of midnight blue, spangled with silver stars, draped both the walls and the table, where their hostess was seated. She herself was startlingly transformed by a voluminous robe and turban of the same material. Spread out before her on the table was a large sheet of parchment, curling at the edges as though very old. Beside it was a globe of crystal, mounted on an ebony stand.

"Go on," whispered the countess from behind him.

Forrest blinked once, then proceeded into the room. "Am I to sit here, ma'am?" he asked blandly as his composure returned, gesturing at the only other chair.

Mrs. Lawrence—or Madame Fortunata now, he supposed—inclined her head regally, and he seated himself across from her. The parchment, he saw, was a chart of the constellations. He had read a fair amount of astronomy at Oxford, but had no idea what the various notations around the stars meant. Something to do with his future, no doubt, he thought cynically.

As if in answer, Madame Fortunata pointed at a group of stars near the top edge of the chart. "This is Taurus, the sign under which you were born," she intoned in a voice markedly different from the one she had used in the parlour. "At the hour of your birth, Venus was in ascendancy and it is she whom we must consult to learn the identity of your soul mate."

"Soul mate?" he echoed incredulously.

"Sshh!" admonished Lady Dearborn from just inside the closed door.

The fortune-teller made no sign that she had heard either of them, but positioned the crystal globe over the parchment and gazed raptly into it. "I see her now. She is tall for a woman and sculpted like the goddess herself. Hair of gold and eyes as blue as the sky."

Madame Fortunata now had Forrest's full attention. "Hair of gold, you say? Always did fancy blondes. Anything else?"

"Quiet and composed, graceful and demure. A vision of loveliness, soon to come to London for the first time. The stars can tell me no more."

"Her name, for instance?" asked Forrest. His scepticism, momentarily shaken, returned in full force. "No doubt there will be quite a few golden-haired, blue eyed debutantes this Season. How am I to know which one is my 'soul mate'?"

Madame Fortunata looked him full in the eyes. "You will know," she said.

"Come, Forrest," broke in the countess. "Did you not say you were expected at White's? Be a dear and send your curricle back for me once you arrive. I wish to stay a bit longer and have my own horoscope read."

The earl started, then turned, having briefly forgotten his mother's presence. "Certainly. I assume we may consider this matter closed?" At her innocent nod, he bowed to both ladies and took his leave.

"You did beautifully, Cora," said Lady Dearborn after the door had closed behind him. "I don't think he suspected a thing."

"I'm glad I was able to find that old crystal. I couldn't think of any other way to manufacture the description you suggested. Are you certain there will be a girl to fit it?" asked Mrs. Lawrence, removing her robe and turban. "I must admit you were right about the golden hair; it certainly made him prick up his ears."

"Dear Forrest has always preferred his, ah, ladies fair, though I doubt he knows that I know it," said the countess with a chuckle. "And never fear, I've not known a Season yet without its share of blond debutantes, by nature or artifice. Trust me to discover which one has the best pedigree and pitch her at him, reminding him all the while of his destiny. Do the stars really predict him to marry this year?"

Mrs. Lawrence frowned at her chart, holding it closer to the candle. "Very possibly," she admitted. "The constellations predict a Season of surprises for the earl, with an emphasis on romance."

"Well, another opera dancer would scarcely be a surprise, so I will assume that means marriage," decided Lady Dearborn with a bob of her turban. "The stars have never steered me wrong yet."

BETWEEN AFTERNOONS at Gentleman Jackson's or the War Office and evenings at cards or the theatre, Lord Dearborn quickly forgot his amusing interlude with Madame Fortunata. He might have shared it with his friends, as a jest that they would undoubtedly enjoy, had he not felt that in relating it he would be opening his mother to their ridicule, as well. Therefore, he did not mention it to anyone, and the matter soon slipped from his mind.

One evening nearly a month later, however, as the Season was just beginning to burst upon London, the incident was recalled vividly to his memory. He was escorting his mother (who had kept her promise in not referring again to his deplorable lack of wife and heirs) to a musicale at Lady Seabrook's when they encountered Mrs. Lawrence. Dressed as she was in a subdued, tasteful evening gown of cream silk, he could not at once remember where he had met the lady before.

"Cora! I am delighted to see you here!" exclaimed the countess, rectifying the lapse in his memory.

"My lady," responded Mrs. Lawrence much more properly, though her smile was as warm as her friend's. "You are looking extremely well."

"Let us sit over here, out of the way, and have a nice cose," suggested Lady Dearborn, taking Mrs. Lawrence's arm. "You will excuse us, of course, Forrest."

The earl nodded, bowing to both ladies before leaving them to their conversation. He walked thoughtfully towards the supper-room, where a lavish buffet was laid out. Seeing Mrs. Lawrence had vividly recalled her predictions to his mind, and he considered them again with a smile.

It was almost a shame, he thought, that her fortune-telling nonsense could not actually order the future. A woman such as she had described—tall, fair, quiet and demure—would be exactly what he might look for in a wife. He had always preferred blondes, something Mrs. Lawrence could not have known, as he was careful to keep his various *affaires* from his mother's ears. As he himself topped six feet, a tall woman would complement him well, he thought. Quiet—yes, he would infinitely prefer that to the mindless chatter most schoolroom misses subjected one to. And demure—a wife who would not be constantly hanging on his sleeve, making endless demands on his attention and purse-strings. Such a female might easily tempt him into parson's mousetrap, he mused.

Unconsciously, Forrest sighed with regret as he allowed the pleasant fantasy to disperse. At thirty, a prime catch since assuming his title at eighteen, he had endured more Seasons, more fluttering debutantes and more matchmaking mamas than he cared to remember. None had come even close to that ideal. Surely it was the sheerest folly to think that just because some fortune-teller had said what she thought he wanted to hear, such a one would magically appear this Season.

Pausing at the door to the supper-room, he shook his head to clear it of such unaccustomed thoughts. It was high time he found another mistress, he decided. He had broken things off with Glorianna nearly a month ago, and had yet to find a replacement for her. Unfulfilled physical desires must surely be the reason for his wayward imagination.

He sighed again. The truth was, he was growing tired of such transient arrangements; he was lonely, in a way no mistress could remedy. *"Soul mate."* Madame Fortunata's words came back to him. There was something strangely attractive in the idea of a woman, one perfect woman, intended solely for him. One who would fill the empty spaces in his life as he would fill those in hers.

Folly! he told himself firmly, putting the idea forcibly from his mind. Forrest gazed around the sumptuously furnished room, diverting his thoughts by inventing fictitious histories for those members of the gathering that he had not yet met. There, consuming lobster patties with relish, was a very young buck who doubtless considered himself a sporting gent, judging by his spotted Belcher neckcloth and the careless set of his coat. The earl smiled to himself, imagining that scrawny figure stripped down at a boxing parlour, looking like a plucked chicken.

His glance travelled across various and sundry newcomers to the social scene, pausing occasionally on a particularly eccentric specimen. The family just entering the room did not fall into that category at first glance: father, sober and respectably clad; mother, a few years younger, handsome in an overstated way; two daughters, one small and dark, not in his style at all, whose dress was at least two years out of mode, and the other...Forrest's gaze sharpened abruptly. Tall, golden-haired and lovely, the other girl definitely required further study.

Advancing carefully towards this vision, the earl made closer observations. The blonde stood perfectly still, her head at a regal angle. Leaning down, she whispered something to the dark girl, who seemed to have a great deal to say in reply. While she spoke, the lady who had captured his attention merely smiled, nodding once or twice. As the group moved into the room, he was struck by the grace of her stride.

His head in a whirl at this sudden materialization of his fanciful day-dream, Forrest approached to seek an introduction to the woman who was clearly his Destiny.

CHAPTER TWO

"EVERYONE LOOKS so *elegant*, Ellie, and there are so many of them!" whispered Rosalind to her companion. "I shall be frightened to death to speak to anyone!"

"Nonsense!" admonished the little brunette. "You are by far the prettiest girl in the room. Anyone with half an eye can see that. Just hold your head up, as your mama is always saying, and accept any compliments as your due. Goodness knows, you deserve them!"

Elinor O'Day regarded her cousin with frank admiration. Rosalind was the most beautiful young lady she could imagine, and her new gown only emphasized the fact. Ellie hoped that Rosalind might be able to fulfil her mother's expectations for her first Season—certainly, life would be miserable for all of them if she didn't!

"Just remember what your gown cost. If that doesn't make you feel elegant, I don't know what will," continued Ellie, and was rewarded by seeing her cousin's back straighten. "That's right. You look just like a princess now. And here comes your first conquest, I'll be bound. See that gentleman approaching, the handsome one with the dark gold hair and black coat?''

Rosalind nodded, though she could not bring herself to look directly at such a frighteningly fashionable gentleman. Instead, she gazed over his shoulder, a properly cool smile frozen on her face. The intimidating man bowed over her mother's hand, introducing himself.

"I perceive you are new to Town. Dearborn, at your service." Forrest managed to keep his eyes off the beauty while greeting her parents.

"I am Mrs. Winston-Fitts, and this is my husband, Emmett," the older woman responded warmly. "It is extremely kind in you, my lord, to make us so welcome at our first function of the Season." Mr. Winston-Fitts acknowledged the greeting, and she continued, "May I present my daughter, Miss Rosalind Winston-Fitts, Lord Dearborn? Oh, yes, and my niece, Miss O'Day."

This last introduction was obviously an afterthought, and the earl scarcely heard it, for on looking at Rosalind as she was introduced, he was dazzled anew. She was even more beautiful at close quarters than she had seemed at a distance, he realized, with her guinea-gold hair, flawless complexion and nobly moulded figure that lacked only a few inches to match his own in height.

"I am charmed to make your acquaintance, Miss Winston-Fitts," he murmured, bowing over her hand without taking his eyes from her face.

"And I yours, my lord," replied Rosalind obediently, her own eyes demurely downcast.

Forrest gazed at her in bemusement for a moment before belatedly recalling his manners. "And yours also, Miss O'Day," he said quickly, meeting the other girl's glance for the first time. He was startled by a distinct flicker of amusement in the clear grey eyes.

"Of course," she replied cryptically, one corner of her mouth quivering upward. "Rosalind was just desiring a glass of ratafia, my lord. If you could be so kind?"

"Certainly! Is there anything else you desire, Miss Winston-Fitts?" he asked solicitously. He was grateful for this chance to demonstrate his professed willingness to serve and bestowed an appreciative smile on the girl who had arranged it. "Or for you, Miss O'Day?" he remembered to ask before making for the table. With another half smile to acknowledge his silent thanks, Ellie shook her head and he departed.

"Ellie, how could you do so? You practically ordered him to bring me a glass of ratafia!" asked Rosalind in an anguished whisper as soon as he was out of earshot.

"Oh, tush!" responded Ellie, also in an undertone lest her aunt overhear. "It was obvious the man was dying to do something to prove his devotion. I merely gave him the chance."

"Devotion! Pray don't tease, Ellie. He has only just met me."

Before Ellie could respond, Mrs. Winston-Fitts spoke. "How fortunate that I was able to introduce you to Lord Dearborn's notice so quickly, my love! He is among the most eligible bachelors in England, and quite elusive, so I hear. I must say, he seemed quite taken with you." She gazed fondly on her beautiful daughter.

"How could he not be?" asked Ellie practically. "Rosalind is looking her absolute best tonight, which is saying a good deal."

"Quite true, Elinor," agreed her aunt. "Even so, you will oblige me by not intruding yourself on any conversation he might strike up with Rosalind." She regarded her niece with less than her usual disfavour, in charity with the world at such unexpected good fortune.

Among the various eligible gentlemen to whom Mrs. Winston-Fitts had hoped to introduce her daughter, Lord Dearborn stood near the top. She had every confidence that Rosalind's beauty, combined with her sizable fortune, would secure her a respectable, nay, spectacular match. Still, it would not do to have Elinor, with her deplorably ready wit, pointing up Rosalind's shyness at every turn.

Elinor knew that her aunt was likely right. Lord Dearborn, or any other suitor, for that matter, would never get to know Rosalind properly if she were always at hand to bail her out of any awkwardness her shyness might create. Glancing over to where the earl stood near the buffet table, Ellie couldn't help thinking that her cousin had done very well on her first evening out. She could scarcely imagine a more handsome gentleman, with his fine physique, antique gold hair and deep, deep blue eyes. What beautiful children he and Rosalind would have together, she mused.

A moment later, Lord Dearborn returned with two glasses. "You might discover yourself thirsty later on," he said in explanation as he handed the second glass to Ellie.

"Thank you, my lord. It is always wise to be prepared against any eventuality," she replied with a twinkle. "I should not wish you to be obliged to make such a journey twice." Then, catching her aunt's slight frown, she forced herself to recede to the background, drifting over to speak to her uncle about a political intrigue she had read of in the papers that morning.

Forrest's glance lingered on Miss O'Day for just the barest moment before returning to Miss Winston-Fitts. "Is the ratafia to your liking?" he asked, hoping to engage her in conversation.

"Yes, thank you, my lord" was all she said, however, before lapsing back into silence.

After watching her for another few moments, he suddenly asked, "Have I a spot on my nose, Miss Winston-Fitts?"

At that, his beautiful companion looked up in startled confusion. "A spot? No, my lord."

"I thought that might be why you so steadfastly avoid looking at me." Though his unexpected question had not made her laugh, as he had hoped, it had at least afforded him his first full glimpse of her eyes. They were wide and guileless, and blue as the sky, just as Madame Fortunata had predicted. The glimpse was fleeting, however, for she dropped her gaze again almost at once.

"Of... of course not," she replied faintly. He waited, but no other response was forthcoming.

"I hope to see you about London, Miss Winston-Fitts," he finally said. "Perhaps you might allow me to show you some of the sights." She nodded, still without looking up, but said nothing. Unable to think of any other ruse to prolong what could hardly be called a conversation, Forrest excused himself. "My mother is waving to me, so I must go to see what she wants. Until next time." He lifted her unresisting hand to his lips in regretful farewell.

"What did I tell you?" asked Ellie, bouncing back to Rosalind's side as soon as he had gone. "He's clearly smitten with you! Aunt Mabel says that he is an earl, and is he not handsome?"

"I suppose so," admitted Rosalind, "though his eyes are not so kind as Sir George's. And he was teasing me, I think. I did not know what to say."

She never did, thought Ellie, around any man other than the aforementioned Sir George. He was but a country squire, however, and not under consideration by Aunt Mabel as a potential husband for her daughter, baronet or no.

"I don't think you needed to say anything, dear," she said comfortingly. "Gentleman like to do most of the talking, I understand. Which is why I frighten them all away!" she added, and had the satisfaction of seeing her cousin smile. "There, that's better. Now here come two or three other gentlemen no doubt desirous of making your acquaintance. What a pity your mama didn't include flirting lessons along with all the others she required you to take!"

"AND WHO, may I ask, is that lovely girl you were just speaking with, Forrest?" asked Lady Dearborn as soon as her son reached her side. "She is quite the prettiest thing I have seen in an age!"

"I was rather taken with her myself, Mother, and would be speaking with her still had you not waved that ridiculous fan in my direction. I've never seen spangles quite so large before. And are those magpie feathers, perchance?"

"Raven," replied the countess with a flick of the said fan that dislodged one of the myriad little black plumes. "You have not answered my question."

"Her name is Miss Rosalind Winston-Fitts, if you must know. And before you point it out, I am very much aware that she admirably fits your Madame Fortunata's description. A connection of hers, perhaps?" As he spoke, he wondered why he had not considered that possibility before.

"Not that I am aware of," returned Lady Dearborn with perfect composure. "I will make enquiries. Not that I can believe Cora capable of so abusing her powers, of course, but we might as well discover what we can about the girl's family." In truth, she was nearly as startled as her son to see how close to the mark Mrs. Lawrence had come, especially since that lady had only been following her own suggestions. However, she was not one to whistle such a golden opportunity down the wind—assuming, of course, that the girl came of an acceptable background. She would indeed make enquiries, and quickly.

"Her father's Christian name is Emmett, if that will be of any help," offered the earl offhandedly. He had a fairly accurate idea of the direction his mother's thoughts were taking and decided that a light tone was in order—for the present, at least.

The countess eyed him shrewdly. "Quite taken with her, eh? Not that I blame you. Who are we mere mortals to struggle against Destiny?"

Forrest snorted, not very convincingly. "I believe I'll go see if there is a hand of whist forming. And if you don't mind, Mother, I'll shape my own destiny." He sauntered off, pointedly in the opposite direction from where Miss Winston-Fitts stood surrounded by half a dozen admirers.

"That's what they all like to believe," Lady Dearborn murmured to his retreating back.

"WELL, EMMETT, was I not right about our Rosalind? There was not another young lady there so admired." Mrs. Winston-Fitts preened visibly over her triumph as they drove back to the Town house they had let for the Season.

Mr. Winston-Fitts withdrew his gaze from the prospect outside the carriage window to regard his wife with cynical amusement. "I don't recall that I ever disputed your judgement in the matter, my dear. No doubt Rosalind is well on her way to securing whatever husband you have selected for her." He returned his attention to the street scene without, refusing to be drawn into another protracted discussion of his daughter's expectations.

"How did you come to be acquainted with Lady Seabrook, Aunt Mabel?" enquired Ellie from the other side of the carriage, nearly as eager as her uncle for a change from the familiar subject.

"Oh, her mother and mine were great friends in their youth," replied Mrs. Winston-Fitts. "Dear Mama moved in the highest circles as a girl, you must know."

Ellie nodded. How could she not know, when Aunt Mabel referred to it at every opportunity? A far less frequent topic of discussion, however, was the fact that her dear mama had married a man of the mercantile persuasion, thereby securing the family fortune—a fortune she would be obliging enough to pass onto her daughter. Mrs. Winston-Fitts had done everything in her power to rectify her mother's social breach by marrying back into the gentry, using that very fortune as her lever. Now, she was determined that Rosalind should take the process a step further by wedding a member of the peerage.

"Who did you like best among the gentlemen you met, Rosalind?" asked Ellie, feeling that her cousin's preferences should have some small bearing on the matter.

"I can hardly tell," replied Rosalind vaguely. "Everyone was so kind."

"Yes, yes, but surely one or two out of the crowd caught your eye," prompted Ellie. "Was there no one you found more handsome than the rest? What of that most attentive Lord Dearborn?" Ellie privately thought that no other gentleman there had come even close to the earl in either appearance or address.

"Yes, he was well enough, I suppose," said Rosalind, "though he did tease. Sir Walter Mansfield was handsome, as well, and not so difficult to understand.''

"Oh, my dear, Sir Walter cannot hold a candle to Dearborn, I assure you,'' interposed Mrs. Winston-Fitts. "Not only is his fortune smaller, but he has far less influence in the government. Lord Dearborn's position is of the highest, as would yours be as his countess.''

Rosalind's blush was visible even in the darkened carriage. "Mama, you go too fast! I have no reason to anticipate an offer from either one of them.''

"One can never begin planning too early for such an eventuality,'' replied her mother loftily. "No husband was ever caught without some little effort on the part of the lady. And Dearborn would be well worth any such effort.''

Rosalind lapsed into an embarrassed silence.

To deflect Aunt Mabel's inevitable lecture on what was expected of her daughter, Ellie said quickly, "Let us not forget, ma'am, that the Season is only just begun. Perhaps Rosalind will catch the eye of a marquess, or even a duke, before it is over.'' Though Ellie could not imagine even a duke comparing with Lord Dearborn, she well knew that if one were to come along, a mere earl would be forgotten—by her aunt, at least.

As she had hoped, her happy suggestion turned Mrs. Winston-Fitts's thoughts to even greater future triumphs and she proceeded to enumerate the eligible peers that Rosalind had not yet met. As she required no response to her monologue, Ellie was free to let her mind wander for the remainder of the drive.

Undoubtedly, many girls in Miss O'Day's position would have envied the beautiful, well-dowered Rosalind, but Ellie felt only a fond protectiveness towards her cousin. From birth, poor Rosalind had been prodded and moulded into her mother's idea of a perfect young lady of fashion, constantly supervised and corrected. She had never experienced the luxury of freedom, which Ellie had taken for granted most of her life—until the coaching accident two years earlier that had killed both her parents.

For the first seventeen years of her life, Ellie had been at liberty to roam the rolling countryside, both in northern England, where she had grown up, and in Ireland, on summer visits to her paternal grandfather. In spite of the endless economies required to stretch an insufficient income, her childhood had been happy, and she had enjoyed the unconditional love of both of her parents, something Rosalind had never really known. Uncle Emmett seemed scarcely to notice his daughter, while his wife doted on Rosalind more for the ambitions she might realize than for herself. To Ellie's way of thinking, it was Rosalind rather than herself who had led an underprivileged life.

Though she had grieved bitterly over the loss of her parents, Ellie could not really repine over her present position as a dependant in the Winston-Fitts household. Even as a poor relation, she lived in greater luxury than she had been accustomed to, and so long as she completed the various chores her aunt assigned her, she enjoyed far more freedom than did Rosalind. Because she had never aspired to the position and fortune that many girls hoped to achieve through marriage, the knowledge that she would now have little chance to attain them did not trouble her.

Suddenly, Lord Dearborn's face arose in her mind's eye. For the first time, she briefly regretted that she lacked the charms to appeal to a man like him. Swiftly, however, she pushed the fleeting notion aside. He seemed most kind, and would doubtless make Rosalind an excellent husband. Surely it was her duty as friend, cousin and companion to do everything in her power to help Rosalind to win him.

CHAPTER THREE

"I'VE DECIDED TO SPEND a few weeks at Huntington Park," announced Lady Dearborn to her son several days later as she took breakfast in her rooms. "The roses will need tending, and I miss my pussies. I'll leave on the morrow, while the crescent moon is still increasing."

Forrest was not surprised. His mother had not spent an entire Season in London in years. Nor could he blame her; their country estate was glorious in the springtime, particularly in comparison to the dirty grey smokiness of the capital city.

"Perhaps I'll join you," he said thoughtfully, deliberately baiting her.

"At the height of the Season?" she exclaimed in shocked accents, just as he had known she would. "'Tis bad enough that I am deserting the fashionable world for the simple life. It would be rank cruelty to deprive the ton of both of us!" Her wink showed that she knew what he was about. "Besides, think of a certain young lady who would be left to the tender mercies of her other gallants."

Forrest's smile broadened. *"Touché,"* he said good-naturedly. "By the by, have your enquiries anent that particular lady borne any fruit?" He had given up trying to conceal his interest in Miss Winston-Fitts from his mother, who was entirely too perceptive. Besides, if he made the girl his wife, as he had nearly decided he would, the countess had every right to know.

"A few pieces, though not yet a full harvest," she replied, sharing the remains of her breakfast with Sapphire, the Siamese cat, who was happily ensconced in her lap. "The Winston-Fittses, as you may already know, are a very old family—older than ours, in fact—and Emmett Winston-Fitts hails from a most respectable branch of it. On *that* side, the girl's blood is as blue as you could wish." She paused, dangling a shred of bacon just out of Sapphire's reach.

"And on the other?" prompted Forrest. He could see that his mother intended dragging out her story for maximum effect, and he had no mind to spend the entire morning listening to it.

Lady Dearborn grimaced slightly. "The mother, I regret to say, was born Mabel Grimes. I have been unable to discover much else about her, but current rumour has her as the daughter of a prosperous textile merchant in or near Birmingham. Her mother, however, was apparently of gentle birth, according to Lady Seabrook, who knew her in her youth. A Miss Wharton. The girl's dowry is quite impressive, by the way."

"No doubt from her maternal grandfather," commented the earl. He was not particularly dismayed, or even surprised, by his mother's disclosures. Miss Winston-Fitts was by no means the first young lady to acquire the financial entreé to Society in such a way.

Forrest knew that the girl's mercantile connections would not dampen his mother's enthusiasm for the match any more than they did his own. Still, he was in no great haste to offer for Miss Winston-Fitts, however lovely she might be. The Season was yet young, and he had scarcely exchanged ten words with her thus far, in spite of dancing twice with her at Mrs. Bullen's rout three nights since. At any rate, he would be foolish to commit himself for life before getting to know her better. He very much looked forward to doing so, in fact.

"Well, ma'am, I know you wouldn't wish me to introduce a cit into the family. You may trust me to keep my handkerchief safely in my pocket." He watched his mother keenly as he casually made this pronouncement.

Struggling up from the chaise in alarm, to the discommodation of Sapphire, the countess hastened to undo the damage. "Nonsense, Forrest! If you care for the girl I will throw no spoke in your wheel on that account, you may be sure. The girl's connections are not generally known, for the mother never mentions that side of her family, and even if they were it would not signify. I can assure you that the Huntington name and the Dearborn title would not suffer in the least from such an alliance." She faltered to a stop as Forrest's grin revealed that he had been bamming her.

"You wretched boy!" she cried. "As if such considerations would weigh with you, anyway. I can't think why you wished me to make enquiries in the first place. It is high time I left London, and you to your own devices." She conveniently forgot that researching Miss Winston-Fitts's background had been her own idea.

"Town will be quite dull without you, ma'am," her son politely assured her, his eyes still twinkling. "But I daresay I will manage somehow to keep myself amused." He rose to go.

"Forrest, wait! I have just had the most delightful idea!" the countess exclaimed suddenly. "Why do we not have a house party at Huntington Park towards the end of the Season? It really does seem most unfair that you should spend the entire spring amidst the dirt of Town while I am enjoying the beauties of the country. Also, I should love to show off my rose gardens to our friends while they are at their best."

"Our friends, or the roses?" asked Forrest teasingly. "A capital idea, however, ma'am. You know that I will seize on any excuse to cut the Season short."

"Excellent! I shall send out invitations as soon as I arrive home. After I greet my poor pussies, that is. They are always so melancholy while I am away, Mrs. Hutchins tells me."

The earl chose not to ask how one might tell when a cat was melancholy, but instead took up his gloves. "I will leave you to your arrangements, ma'am. The house is sure to be turned topsy-turvy with your packing and I would as lief be out of it. At any rate, if I do not take my morning ride soon, it will no longer be morning."

"Off with you, then," said Lady Dearborn cheerfully. "I'll be leaving by nine tomorrow, so do you be certain to be awake to see me off and to throw a shoe after me for luck."

"You see me your servant, as always, ma'am." With an exaggerated bow, the earl departed his mother's rooms.

AT THAT MOMENT, which lacked nearly an hour till noon, all was yet quiet at the Winston-Fitts Town house. Ellie O'Day stood by the window of her small chamber gazing thoughtfully down at the tiny patch of garden behind the house, going over the day's schedule in her mind while waiting for the rest of the family to bestir themselves.

After breakfast, if such it could properly be called at twelve o'clock, she, Rosalind and Aunt Mabel would once again venture out to the shops in their seemingly endless quest for the perfect gown for this or that upcoming function. In particular, her aunt wished to have everything and everyone in readiness for the dinner party she was giving next week. Ellie wondered idly whether her aunt's attention to detail would extend to a new gown for herself, or if she would be obliged to wear another of Rosalind's cast-offs, hemmed and taken in to fit her more diminutive figure. Not that it would bother her, she reminded herself. Rosalind's old gowns were vastly more fashionable than anything she had ever owned before coming to live with the Winston-Fittses.

A scratch at the door interrupted Ellie's thoughts. "Ellie, are you awake?" came Rosalind's voice from without.

Ellie quickly bounded across the little room and flung open the door. "Good morning, Rosie! Are you

ready for another day of fittings?'' she asked her
cousin cheerily.

Rosalind entered the chamber more slowly and sat
on the threadbare pink chair that occupied the mea-
gre space between bed and dressing-table. "I had no
idea I would need so many clothes in London!" she
said with a sigh. "It seems a shocking waste of money
to me."

"I can't think where you acquired your tendency to
economy, Rosie," said Ellie, with a laugh, settling next
to her on the green counterpane of the bed. "Certainly not from Aunt Mabel!"

"Oh, Mama can be thrifty enough when she
chooses," replied Rosalind with uncharacteristic cynicism. "She certainly did not overextend herself on
your room, here or at home." She glanced about at the
tiny chamber and its mismatched furnishings with a
small frown. "If it were not for Papa, she might well
have tried to house you in the garret."

Ellie chuckled again. "You must not think I mind,
truly. Though a garret would be more romantic, don't
you think? Do not all the novel heroines live in one
before their Prince Charming appears?"

But Rosalind had apparently rehearsed what she
meant to say and would not be dissuaded. "Still, I
hope to persuade her to buy you a new gown today.
You might as well make the most of being in London,
and a new gown could be just the thing to attract a
gentleman."

"Your mother will hardly thank me if I lure away
any of your suitors," Ellie pointed out, though the

very thought of any man looking at her while Rosalind was in the same room struck her as absurd.

"I cannot very well marry all of them," said Rosalind, her troubled tone implying that she would far rather not marry any of them. "Besides, I am certain you do not wish to remain dependent on Mama and Papa forever."

Rosalind's perceptiveness rather surprised Ellie. Her cousin, while sweet-natured and affectionate, could not generally be said to possess an understanding of the first order. What she said was true, however; Ellie knew that her post as Aunt Mabel's drudge would become far more irksome once Rosalind left for a home of her own.

"Don't worry, Rosie," she said after a brief pause. "If some duke does not carry me off to his castle this Season, I can always go to my grandfather in Ireland."

"Lord Kerrigan? Have you finally heard from him, then?" Rosalind was momentarily diverted from her purpose.

"Well, no," honesty forced her to say. "I've only had the one letter from my uncle, Lord Clairmont, his heir. That was shortly after my parents . . ." She swallowed before continuing. "He said then that my grandfather was ill, but surely he'd have written again if he had died. Grandfather always had a fondness for me and, ill or not, he would allow me to live at Kerribrooke, I feel certain." Her grey eyes took on a dreamy, faraway expression that made her look almost beautiful as she remembered the picturesque estate in Ireland where she had spent so many childhood summers.

"Still, I think it would be even better if one of the kind gentlemen we have met were to offer for you," said Rosalind, returning doggedly to her plan. "However would you find a husband in the wilds of Ireland?"

"You have been listening too much to your mother, Rosie," admonished Ellie. "I do not consider marriage the be-all and end-all to life, as she does."

Rosalind regarded her with a certain wistfulness. "Well, if you do not go to Ireland and you don't wish to marry, you can stay with me after I do, as my companion. In truth, Ellie, I am not certain I could manage without you!"

Ellie thought of Rosalind married to Lord Dearborn, still the most favoured (by Aunt Mabel, at least) of her suitors, with herself in the role of a dependant in his household. Slowly, she shook her head. "It is sweet of you to say so, Rosie, but I think not. I shall enjoy my vicarious London Season and dance at your wedding, and then I shall go to Kerribrooke. It is the wisest course, I think."

"MAMA, WOULD NOT THIS primrose silk look lovely on Ellie?" asked Rosalind later that day in an effort to fulfil her earlier promise. "It would set off her dark hair admirably."

Mrs. Winston-Fitts turned from her inspection of some new French laces. "Whyever would she need such a gown?" she asked in some irritation. Elinor was not in her good graces at the moment, for she had done a very poor job on an embroidered edging for one of Rosalind's new gowns. She had forgotten, when she had asked her niece to do it, that needlework was by no means Elinor's strong suit.

"Why, she could wear it to our dinner party next week," said Rosalind reasonably. "It will be her formal introduction to Society, you know, as well as mine."

This reminder that the Town house they were renting for the Season possessed no ballroom failed to sweeten her mother's mood. She would dearly have loved to present her dazzling Rosalind properly, at her own come-out ball. "She can wear your yellow silk, if you are so certain the colour will become her. It is too tight for you, anyway," she said sourly.

"Oh, that would be lovely," said Ellie, sorting through a box of buttons at the counter. "You know I have always admired that gown, Rosie."

"Rosalind, if you please, Elinor," admonished her aunt. "I will thank you to limit your use of vulgar nicknames to the house. Ah, yes," she continued in a completely different tone, turning to the modiste as she approached, "that sky blue velvet will make a perfect habit for my daughter, Madame Francine."

"A riding habit?" asked Rosalind in dismay, completely forgetting Ellie for the moment. "Mama, you know I do not ride."

"Tush, anyone can ride. You had lessons as a child. At any rate, you must, for I have recently discovered that Lord Dearborn rides in the Park almost every morning at eleven o'clock. 'Twill be the perfect opportunity to further your acquaintance with him.''

Rosalind looked stricken, and Ellie, well aware of Rosalind's fear of riding, was moved to speak. "'Twill not be so bad, my dear,'' she said soothingly. "No one goes above a trot in the Park, I have heard, and you know you can manage that.'' Ellie hoped that this reassurance might bolster her cousin's spirits; she herself dearly loved to ride. Trying not to sound too eager, she enquired of her aunt, "Will I be expected to accompany her, ma'am?''

"Why, yes, I suppose you must,'' replied Mrs. Winston-Fitts, regarding her closely. Ellie kept her expression carefully neutral. "You ride well, as I recall, and may give Rosalind a few pointers. Lord Dearborn is a first-rate whip, and will doubtless prefer a girl who is at ease on her mount.'' She gave her daughter a significant glance.

Rosalind suddenly smiled as an idea struck her. "Then you will have to buy Ellie a habit as well, Mama, since I have no old one to pass on to her.''

Mrs. Winston-Fitts grimaced, but she was neatly caught and she knew it. "Very well.'' Turning back to the modiste, she said, "Have this velvet made up for my daughter and show us something in wool for my niece, if you please, Madame Francine.''

THREE DAYS LATER, Ellie and Rosalind prepared for their first ride in Hyde Park. Rosalind looked absolutely divine in her new habit, Ellie thought, with the pale blue velvet just matching her eyes. She could not be displeased with her own appearance, either, for while her habit was of wool rather than the more fashionable velvet, the deep peach colour with chocolate brown frogging set off her pale skin and dark hair admirably.

"Aunt Mabel said that I might select our mounts, so we might as well step round to the mews ourselves. 'Twill be quicker than having a succession of horses brought to the door for our inspection," said Ellie as she finished tying the dark blue ribands on Rosalind's sky blue shako hat. She herself was wearing her usual chip straw bonnet.

"To the mews? Ourselves?" asked Rosalind uncertainly. "Is that quite proper?"

"I can't see why not. It is not as though we are going to Tattersall's, and the stable is just round the corner behind the garden."

Ellie was correct. After only a few minutes walking, the two young ladies, accompanied by a footman, entered the warm dimness of the boarding stables on Market Mews behind Curzon Street. Ellie breathed in the pungent equine scent with relish, but Rosalind coughed at the unfamiliar smell.

"Miss Winston-Fitts! Miss O'Day!" exclaimed the groom in surprise when he saw them. "I had a pair of horses all ready to lead round to the front door as soon as the missus sent word."

"We decided to look at the horses ourselves," replied Ellie calmly. In truth, she had feared that they would be mounted on slugs otherwise. That might be well enough for Rosalind, but she intended to select a beast with some spirit, if one could possibly be had.

"Certainly, miss, right this way," said the groom, leading them to a selection of four or five riding horses. To Ellie's delight, she recognized the spunky little mare she had ridden in Birmingham before the family's removal to London.

"They brought Firefly along! Saddle her for me please, William," she directed the groom. "And I think Molly will do well for Miss Winston-Fitts, won't she, Rosie?"

Rosalind nodded dubiously. "I rode her once before, did I not?" she asked, eyeing the large chestnut mare.

"Yes, and you stayed on perfectly well," Ellie reminded her. "Here, give her a carrot and she will remember you, too." She seized one from a bin behind her. "Hold your hand flat, like that. Right."

"Her nose is so soft!" exclaimed Rosalind in surprise after the carrot had disappeared in one loud crunch.

"Go ahead and stroke it. Molly won't bite," Ellie assured her. She was doing the same with Firefly, becoming reacquainted with her favourite mount. She wondered if her uncle had arranged to have her brought to London; he occasionally surprised her with such evidences of thoughtfulness, she thought with a smile. Just then, she felt something rubbing against her skirts and looked down.

"Where did you come from, kitty?" she asked, reaching down to stroke the calico cat at her feet.

"Look, Rosie, isn't she precious?" she said to her cousin, picking up the cat.

To her surprise, Rosalind blanched and backed away. "Oh! Send it away, Ellie, please! I vow, cats frighten me to death!"

"Goodness, I had no idea." Ellie quickly set the cat back on the straw. "Go on, kitty, shoo!" she said, gently nudging it away from Rosalind with her foot. The cat took the hint and went to dig through a pile of hay, no doubt in search of mice. "I'm sorry, Rosie."

"You . . . you could not know," said Rosalind, her colour slowly returning. "My mother hates cats, and I have been afraid of them since I was a little girl. I'm not really certain why."

"Doubtless something Aunt Mabel told you about them when you were young," theorized Ellie. "Never mind. I promise not to put one in your face again. Ah! Here are our horses."

The groom helped them into their saddles before mounting the gelding he would ride to accompany them to the Park. Closely watching her cousin's inexpert riding, Ellie had no time to wonder why her own heart was fluttering at the thought of encountering Lord Dearborn there.

CHAPTER FOUR

IT WAS A SPARKLING May morning, newly opened flowers wafting their scents on the gentle breeze while remnants of dew glinted in the sunshine. A perfect morning for a ride, thought Forrest as he urged his roan gelding to a brisk hand canter. Hyde Park was the most pleasant corner of London, in his opinion, particularly in the spring, though it was still a far cry from his own Huntington Park. In less than a month he would be back home, however, thanks to his mother's planned house party.

Idly, he wondered how Miss Winston-Fitts would like his country estate. He tried to envisage the delight on her face when she first beheld the rambling manor house with its mullioned windows and climbing ivy, but failed utterly. The only expression he could recall seeing her wear was one of shy politeness. Not that that detracted from her charm, he told himself hastily. No, it simply added a becoming modesty to her other sterling qualities—most desirable in a wife, surely.

Turning his horse to canter back in the direction of the Park gates, he looked up to see the object of his devotion just entering them, along with her cousin—

what was her name? Miss O'Something—and a groom. The earl urged his mount faster.

"Well met, ladies," he called out, executing a neat half bow from the saddle. "You make a lovely morning even more beautiful." His gaze lingered on Rosalind, who he thought looked positively celestial in her sky blue habit.

As usual, Rosalind merely murmured her thanks at the compliment without meeting the earl's glance, leaving it to Ellie to fill the gap. "That's a prime-looking animal, my lord. Your taste in horseflesh is to be commended."

"Why, thank you," he replied, furiously trying to remember her name. "Your mare appears to have excellent lines, as well." He looked at the horse rather than the girl, vaguely embarrassed.

"Yes, Firefly goes very nicely," she agreed. "Of course, I can take no credit for that, as my uncle purchased her before I joined the family."

Lord Dearborn noticed how tactfully she refrained from mentioning her circumstances, though he had formed a fairly accurate opinion of what they must be. He turned back to Miss Winston-Fitts, and all thoughts of her companion fled at once.

"I was just about to do the circuit. Dare I hope that you ladies will honour me with your company?"

"We . . . would be delighted, my lord," replied Rosalind timidly, after a prompting glance from Ellie.

The path would have accommodated three comfortably, but Ellie forced herself to rein back behind Lord Dearborn and her cousin, mindful of her aunt's strictures. From that vantage point, she had ample opportunity to examine the earl and to conclude that he was indeed as handsome as she had remembered. Though he had spoken to and danced with Rosalind at the two or three evening entertainments they had attended during the past week, Ellie had not been face to face with him since that first occasion at Lady Seabrook's.

Well aware that her overt inspection was improper, but equally aware that neither he nor Rosalind were likely to observe it, Ellie continued it unabashedly, noting that Lord Dearborn sat his horse very well. Unfortunately, the same could not be said for her cousin; Rosalind looked uncomfortable in the extreme, as though there were a burr between her and the saddle. Ellie prayed that Lord Dearborn might be too bemused by Rosalind's face to notice her poor seat.

"Have you a problem with your mount, Miss Winston-Fitts?" he asked a moment later. "She is not coming up lame, is she?"

"I—I don't believe so, my lord," said Rosalind, flushing scarlet.

Ellie nudged Firefly forward. "Rosalind has not ridden in some time, my lord," she interposed quickly. "We took a roundabout way to the Park, and doubtless she is beginning to feel a bit stiff."

Rosalind shot her a grateful glance, but Lord Dearborn was all concern. "Then you must dismount immediately, Miss Winston-Fitts, and walk with me for a short distance. That is the surest way to avoid soreness."

Rosalind dismounted eagerly, obviously glad of any excuse to be on the ground again. Ellie bit her lip, vexed at herself for having provided an opportunity for her cousin to be more private with the earl. Quickly, though, she caught herself up. Why ever should she be vexed? Did she not want Aunt Mabel's plan to succeed? After all, she had already decided that Lord Dearborn would make Rosalind a better husband than any of her other suitors, and her first wish must be for her cousin's happiness—mustn't it?

Ellie and the groom, still mounted, followed the couple at a slow walk, near enough to preserve propriety but far enough back to allow them to converse privately. As far as Ellie could tell, however, they did not appear to be talking at all. She let out a sigh of amused exasperation. How did Rosalind expect to attach the earl's interest if she would not even speak to the man? Poor Rosalind was simply too shy for her own good, Ellie thought. She wondered if there were any encouragement she could offer her cousin that Aunt Mabel had not already tried a hundred times.

"The Park is lovely this time of year," commented Lord Dearborn after he and Miss Winston-Fitts had walked for several minutes in silence. It was patently obvious to him that she would not take the initiative in starting any conversation.

"Yes, my lord," agreed Rosalind, as usual.

"Do you go to Lady Sefton's ball tonight?" he asked. He doubted not that her mother, at least, had been in raptures at an invitation from the esteemed patroness of Almack's, an invitation that he had been instrumental in arranging.

"Yes, my lord," replied Rosalind, still not meeting his eye. "I—I am looking forward to it immensely," she added, apparently feeling that something more was called for.

"I, too, especially now that I know you will be there," said the earl gallantly, causing Rosalind to blush slightly. As always when he complimented her, she appeared charmingly flustered, and he knew he would get nothing further out of her. After a moment, he asked if she felt equal to remounting.

Rosalind hesitated, for all the world as if she would rather not. "I—I suppose so, my lord," she finally said.

"I do hope you will not be too stiff to dance the first set with me tonight, Miss Winston-Fitts," he said with a smile that held a hint of concern. She must be sore indeed to be so reluctant to ride.

"Oh, no. That is, I—I'm certain any stiffness will have worn off by then, my lord," responded Rosalind in some confusion. Flushing again, she allowed him to assist her back into the saddle.

"Shall we continue our ride?" asked Ellie brightly once they were reassembled. "Rosalind is looking much more the thing, don't you think, my lord?"

As she had intended, Lord Dearborn was obliged to regard her cousin closely before replying. "Very much so, I should say," he said warmly.

Ellie felt a twinge of something that might have been annoyance, but she thrust it firmly aside without examination. No doubt exercise would settle her conflicting feelings. "Let us proceed, then. Firefly is getting quite restive." Without waiting for a reply, she urged the bay mare into a quick trot, leaving the others to follow as they would.

ELLIE SIGHED at her reflection in the glass. For once, she wished that she were handy with a needle, that she might have added a flounce or some edging to the simple pearl-grey gown.

"Pish, what are you mooning about?" she asked her reflection aloud. "The gown is silk, is it not? And it even matches your eyes. How can it possibly matter to you that Rosie wore it in the country last fall?"

Besides, she thought, as she descended the stairs to await the rest of the family, Aunt Mabel had had her own mantua maker alter it, so it fit her much better than most of her other gowns, which she had been forced to hem and take in herself. And her hair had been newly cut and fashionably arranged, curling about her ears. She had absolutely no cause for complaint.

Still, she could not suppress a small pang of envy when she saw Rosalind a few minutes later looking like an angel in a confection of pink and white. Ellie had never been one to pay particular heed to her own appearance, but it was difficult not to compare the vision before her to the image that had so recently confronted her in her own mirror.

"You look wonderful, Rosie," she said quite honestly. "The gentlemen will all be quite dazzled."

"I trust they will be," said Mrs. Winston-Fitts, descending the stairs at that moment. "She does look well, doesn't she?" She regarded her daughter complacently.

To Ellie's surprise, Rosalind ignored her mother. "I wish you could have had a new gown, Ellie," she said, "but I must admit that one becomes you far better than it did me. Your skin positively glows against that silvery grey.''

Mrs. Winston-Fitts directed a sharp glance at her niece, but was apparently reassured by what she saw. "You will do, Elinor" was all she said. Then, as her husband took his place beside her, "The carriage is waiting, girls. Remember everything I told you, pray.''

Lest they had forgotten since that afternoon, Mrs. Winston-Fitts repeated every one of her lengthy list of instructions during the brief drive to Lady Sefton's house, impressing on them again the honour that was being done them by this invitation. Her uncle's occasional cynical insertions to his wife's lecture kept Ellie from feeling overcome, but poor Rosalind looked frightened to death, she thought.

"And, finally, do not forget to thank our hostess as we are leaving," Aunt Mabel said as their carriage rolled to the head of the queue before the front door. "And remember to curtsy!" she whispered loudly as a footman opened the door and let down the steps.

Ellie nodded absently, looking up in awe at the impressive edifice they were about to enter. It was easily three or four times the size of the Winston-Fittses' Town house, she thought. Her wonderment increased as she followed her aunt and uncle inside. Their hostess awaited her guests at the top of a broad marble staircase, which led into the sumptuously appointed ballroom.

"Mr. and Mrs. Winston-Fitts, Miss Winston-Fitts, Miss O'Day," intoned the rigidly formal butler.

By way of contrast, however, Lady Sefton greeted them warmly, exclaiming over Rosalind's beauty with a sincerity that set both girls at ease. Ellie was grateful for her kindness, for she had feared that Rosalind might faint dead away after her mother's terrifying admonishments.

"Charming, my dear," said Lady Sefton as Ellie rose from her curtsy. "I daresay you will set a new fashion. You have your mother's eyes, I see."

Ellie blinked in surprise. "Why, thank you, my lady." Her mother had known Lady Sefton? Before she could probe for more information, the countess swept them on into the ballroom.

"Now, run along and join the young people," she said with a smile. "I so hope you will enjoy my little gathering."

Ellie had to stifle a laugh when she turned to face the "little gathering." As one of the patronesses of Almack's and hostess of the first major ball of the Season, Lady Sefton had attracted nearly all the fashionable world to her home for the evening, or so it appeared.

"I had wondered what was meant when a party was described as a 'crush,'" she confided to Rosalind, who was looking rather pale. "Now I know." Glancing up, she caught her aunt's speculative gaze.

"You did not tell me your mother was acquainted with Lady Sefton," Mrs. Winston-Fitts said accusingly.

"I did not know it myself, Aunt Mabel," she replied. "Mama rarely spoke about her two Seasons in London and I never thought to ask."

"Hmph," snorted her aunt, turning away. "There is Lord Dearborn, Rosalind, my love. Did you not say you are promised to him for the first dance?"

In spite of herself, Ellie looked in the direction indicated by her aunt, and her heart gave an unsettling thump. The earl was looking exceptionally handsome in his evening dress of black tails and knee breeches, his deep gold hair waving carelessly above the strong, patrician brow and piercing blue eyes. She simply *must* not develop a *tendre* for the man, Ellie told herself. He was to be Rosalind's, and she would simply have to remember that fact.

Not that he was likely to let her forget it, she thought wryly a moment later, as she watched him bowing solicitously over Rosalind's hand. Ellie could not in the least understand her cousin's continued coolness towards the earl. How could her heart not melt in the face of that charming smile? But Rosalind looked as uncomfortable as she always did in his presence.

Lord Dearborn led Rosalind onto the floor for the first set, which happened to be a country dance. Watching her cousin from the sidelines, Ellie noted with approval that Rosalind had apparently remembered their dancing instructor's lessons perfectly. She was not conversing with her partner, but that was hardly surprising, given the nature of the dance. Ellie seriously doubted, however, that Rosalind would manage more than monosyllables even were they dancing the waltz. Ruthlessly, Ellie forced down the tiny pang that assailed her at the thought of her cousin waltzing with Lord Dearborn. Really, this would not do at all!

To distract herself from the dancers, Ellie turned to survey the entrance, watching with interest as guest after guest arrived to join the burgeoning throng. There was Lady Seabrook, whom they had met on their first evening out, in a splendid gown of peacock blue. Little Lord Seabrook, at her side, looked rather like a penguin in comparison, she thought, standing stiffly in his black-and-white evening wear.

Ellie mused similarly over each of the arriving guests, a few of whom were known to her but most of whom were not. The steady stream was slowing to a trickle as the first set drew to a close, and Ellie sighed as she started to turn away. Just then, however, a familiar face drew her attention back to the door.

Gracious! she thought. Was that not Sir George Bellamy, the Winston-Fittses' neighbour from Warwickshire? Now, who would have thought that he would come to London for the Season? Ellie clearly recalled his saying, during a dinner at the Winston-Fittses' last year, that he detested all of the hurly-burly of Town. But there was no mistaking that stocky figure and plain, honest face, or the unruly shock of sandy hair. Ellie stepped forward eagerly.

"Sir George!" she exclaimed. "What a pleasant surprise. I thought you never came to London."

"Miss O'Day! I am delighted to see you again. You are looking well." He bowed solemnly over her hand. "This particular Season holds a certain attraction for me," he continued somewhat self-consciously, his eyes going past her to the dance floor, where the set was just breaking up.

Ellie followed his gaze, wondering unhappily if she ought to warn him of her aunt's plans for Rosalind. Sir George had been more or less courting her cousin in his slow, steady way before they had left for London but had never gone so far as to declare himself. Ellie liked Sir George, and did not relish the prospect of seeing him hurt.

"Sir George," she began, but at that moment Rosalind emerged from the crowded dance floor on Lord Dearborn's arm.

Ellie thought she looked breathtaking, slightly flushed from her recent exertions, though her face was a bit anxious as she scanned the throng near the door, trying to locate her parents. Suddenly, Rosalind's glance fell on Sir George, and the change in her expression was remarkable. Her eyes sparkled and her cheeks grew very pink as the first truly happy smile Ellie had seen her wear since reaching London lit up her face.

"Sir George!" she cried almost rapturously. "Is it really you?" For a moment, Ellie thought her cousin was actually going to fling herself into his arms, but apparently Rosalind remembered where she was in time. "I—I mean, I am delighted to see you in Town," she finished lamely, stopping a few feet from the squire.

Ellie glanced uneasily at Lord Dearborn, whom Rosalind had quite obviously forgotten, and saw that he was wearing a small, thoughtful frown.

"Sir George Bellamy, may I introduce Lord Dearborn?" she said quickly, in an effort to retrieve the situation. At that moment, Mrs. Winston-Fitts returned from the floor, her husband in tow.

"Sir George," she said coolly. "What a pleasure." She offered her hand to the newcomer, while Mr. Winston-Fitts echoed her sentiments with far greater warmth. "I trust you have met Lord Dearborn? Good. Perhaps you would be so kind as to fetch me a glass of orgeat, and then you can catch me up on all of the news from the country."

Sir George, however, was not to be so easily dissuaded from his objective. "I would be delighted, ma'am, as soon as I secure a dance with Miss Winston-Fitts, if her card is not already full."

Rosalind stepped forward eagerly, but her mother forestalled her.

"I fear it likely is, Sir George," she said quickly. "Our Rosalind has quite taken London by storm. But we shall be delighted to see you at the dinner party I am giving on Thursday."

Thus dismissed, Sir George had no recourse but to make his way to the refreshment table to procure the requested orgeat, pausing first to direct a lingering glance at Rosalind with his kind brown eyes, a glance that was returned with equal warmth. Lord Dearborn did not miss the exchange and wore a pensive expression as he excused himself to claim his next partner.

CHAPTER FIVE

"MAMA, HOW COULD YOU say that?" demanded Rosalind with a spirit that startled both of her parents and Ellie, as well. "You know perfectly well that I am not engaged for every dance, and I think it was odious of you to send poor Sir George off like that with a flea in his ear, especially as he only just arrived in Town!"

Mrs. Winston-Fitts gaped at her darling daughter's unwonted outburst, but quickly gathered her wits enough to say, "I did no such thing. I merely asked the man to fetch me a glass of orgeat. There was nothing in the least uncivil about it."

"Perhaps we can make it up by allowing him a dance with Rosalind later on," suggested her husband, his dark eyes twinkling. Ellie glanced at Uncle Emmett, trying to divine his thoughts and, as usual, failing utterly. Could it be that he favoured Sir George's suit, or was he merely trying to set up Aunt Mabel's back she wondered. One seemed as likely as the other.

Mrs. Winston-Fitts clearly did not care for her husband's suggestion, but gave in ungraciously. "Oh, very well, if that is what you wish. He is a neighbour, after all."

"And a very old friend," agreed Mr. Winston-Fitts. "That is settled, then."

"I'll put him down for the fourth, then, for I am already engaged for the next two," said Rosalind happily. As she finished speaking, her next partner, Viscount Montforth, came to claim her. At once, she was her usual, tongue-tied self. Ellie watched her cousin depart for the dance floor, marvelling at the change she had just witnessed in her. She had known Sir George had a fondness for Rosalind—indeed, all the neighbourhood had known it—but she had never suspected that Rosalind returned his feelings. Perhaps Rosalind was merely homesick, and welcomed a familiar face from Warwickshire, but to Ellie it had appeared to be more than that.

When Sir George returned with Mrs. Winston-Fitts's orgeat a few minutes later, he bowed formally to Ellie, requesting that she grant him the next dance. She agreed at once.

"Thank you, Sir George, I should be delighted. If you would still care for a dance with my cousin, she has discovered that she has the next one after that free, after all." She was not about to allow her aunt to renege on her promise.

The portly squire's face lit up, making him almost handsome. "How marvellous!" he said. But then, ever the gentleman, he turned his whole attention to his current partner. "Shall we, Miss O'Day?" He extended his arm.

Ellie inclined her head in mock formality and accompanied him to the floor, where the next set was forming. The movements of the dance did not allow much opportunity for conversation, but Sir George did manage to ask her at one point whether Miss Winston-Fitts was yet betrothed. Ellie was able to reassure him on that point and was dismayed by the expression of relief that spread across Sir George's earnest countenance. She wished she could envisage as much hope for his suit as he apparently did.

Lord Dearborn was standing near the Winston-Fittses when Ellie and Rosalind returned from the floor, engaging them in desultory conversation. Upon learning that Rosalind was engaged to Sir George for the next dance, he gallantly turned to Ellie with an elegant bow.

"Will you do me the honour, Miss O'Day?" he asked.

Ellie knew it was simple politeness that prompted him to ask, but her heart began to beat faster nonetheless. "Thank you, my lord," she replied, no more able to come up with a witty remark than her cousin. To further her agitation, the orchestra struck up the strains of a waltz.

Without hesitation, Lord Dearborn swept her into the dance, and Ellie discovered that he made an excellent partner. She followed his steps effortlessly, meanwhile desperately trying to think of something inconsequential to say. It was not in her nature to remain silent for long.

"I see you were able to recall my name, my lord," she finally said, glancing up at him. She would *not* let him see how he unsettled her!

His brows rose. "Are you implying that I had forgotten it?" he asked, the glint in his eyes daring her to pursue the topic.

"In the Park this morning, I could not help but notice how studiously you avoided addressing me directly," she told him. "I found it more comfortable to suppose you had forgotten my name than that you found me such an antidote that you could not bear to look at me."

The earl regarded her in surprise for a moment, then began to chuckle. "I can scarcely deny it now, can I, Miss O'Day? Very well, I confess. Your uncle had just refreshed my memory before I led you out. Are you satisfied at forcing me to admit to such a *faux pas* as forgetting a lady's name?"

"Perfectly," she replied, grey eyes twinkling. He gazed down at her speculatively for a moment, the beginnings of an answering twinkle in his own deep blue eyes, but said nothing.

They danced in silence for a few moments, then, "Who is that Bellamy fellow?" asked the earl abruptly.

Ellie blinked up at him. "Sir George? He is the squire of the district in Warwickshire where the Winston-Fittses live, on the outskirts of Birmingham."

"Ah." Lord Dearborn nodded. "Miss Winston-Fitts seemed deuced glad to see him," he commented after a brief pause.

Ellie regarded him cautiously. Would the thought of a rival cool his ardour for Rosalind, or increase it? she wondered. And which ought she to hope for? "He is a great friend of the family," she said noncommittally. "Rosalind has known him since she was a child." He might draw what conclusions he would from that; she would neither confirm nor deny his obvious suspicion.

"I see." The earl said nothing more for the remainder of their waltz, beyond politely expressing his pleasure in dancing with her at its conclusion.

"And I thank you, my lord," said Ellie in response. "It was kind in you to take pity on a wallflower."

"Never that, Miss O'Day, surely," he replied, with another searching look at her. "Perhaps you will honour me again before the evening is over."

"Perhaps," said Ellie, lifting her chin. Surely, she thought in sudden alarm, he did not think she had been angling for another dance? If he did ask, she doubted her ability to refuse him.

The earl merely bowed, however, and moved off in search of whatever young lady he was promised to for the next set. Ellie breathed a sigh of relief. What was it about Lord Dearborn that caused her wits to go a-begging?

As THE EVENING PROGRESSED, Ellie was surprised to find herself by no means without partners. Though she had no doubt that most of them offered to lead her out only upon discovering that Rosalind's card was full—as it was by the fifth set—she nevertheless enjoyed herself immensely. It seemed no time at all had passed before the supper dance arrived at midnight. Glancing at the card dangling from her wrist, Ellie was amazed to discover that all her remaining dances were spoken for. Sir George had requested the supper dance, she recalled, after finding that Lord Dearborn had already engaged Rosalind for that set.

"Miss O'Day! Here you are," puffed Sir George, hurrying up at that moment. "It is so crowded in here that one can scarce breathe, let alone find anyone."

Not surprisingly, the orchestra struck up another waltz for the couples who would be going in to supper together. Though he concealed it quickly, Ellie noticed the regret that passed fleetingly across Sir George's face and knew that he was wishing that it were Rosalind instead of herself he held in his arms. The thought did not offend her in the least, however; as a matter of fact, on catching sight of Rosalind and Lord Dearborn dancing together on the far side of the room, she found she heartily shared his wish.

"I hear that Lady Sefton is famous for her supper table," she said in an attempt to divert Sir George's thoughts, as well as her own. "I vow, I am quite famished after all this exercise."

Sir George made a courteous reply, and they determinedly conversed on that topic and others equally safe until the music ceased. Passing through the archway to where the tables for supper were set out, they found most of the seats already taken. Glancing around in hopes of spotting someone she knew, Ellie saw Rosalind seated alone at a table for four, motioning eagerly to them. Without stopping to consult her escort, Ellie moved at once in her direction.

"Do please join us, Ellie, Sir George," said Rosalind eagerly as they drew near. Ellie noticed that her colour was unusually high. "Lord Dearborn has already gone to fetch plates from the buffet."

"I shall do likewise, then," said Sir George, after a courtly bow to Rosalind.

"Thank heavens you are to sit with me, Ellie," whispered Rosalind as Sir George trotted off in the direction of the heavily laden buffet tables. "I was ready to sink at the idea of trying to think of things to say to Lord Dearborn all through supper." Then, after a slight pause, "Sir George is looking well, don't you think?"

"He certainly is," agreed Ellie, hiding a smile. "Many of the young ladies here tonight have seemed to think so." She watched her cousin closely as she made the seemingly offhand remark.

Rosalind paled slightly, causing Ellie to despise herself at once. "Have...have they?" Rosalind asked in an almost stricken voice. "Has he danced with very many of them, then?"

"No, dear, I was teasing," said Ellie quickly. "He has danced very little, that I could see, and seems to have spent most of the evening following you with his eyes." It was a mystery to Ellie how her cousin could possibly prefer the plump, prosaic Sir George over the dashing Lord Dearborn, but that she did was plain. Rosalind's next statement enlightened her.

"I feel so...so *safe* around Sir George," she confessed, her eyes revealing her relief at Ellie's words. "He never teases, or flirts, or says things that I have to decipher for double meanings."

Ellie had to agree that there was certainly nothing the least bit threatening about Sir George. Feeling safe with a man was not precisely the same thing as being in love with him, however. Before she could put that thought into words, the gentlemen returned to the table bearing plates overflowing with delicacies. Lady Sefton's reputation was well deserved, it appeared.

Lord Dearborn had struck up a conversation with Sir George on the way back to the table in hopes of discovering more about his unlikely rival. He had not been deceived by Miss O'Day's vague answers to his questions earlier. It had been patently obvious that Miss Winston-Fitts regarded the man as more than an old family friend. He wondered for a moment about Miss O'Day's motives in hiding her cousin's *tendre* for the squire from him. Most likely, they were the same as her aunt's—to secure the better match, namely himself, for the beauteous Rosalind.

In spite of his intention to dislike Sir George Bellamy, the earl quickly found that the man was perfectly pleasant and polite, with none of the toad-eating tendencies he might have expected from a country squire newly arrived in Town. Sir George's manner was natural and his conversation sensible, if not particularly stimulating. Lord Dearborn decided to probe deeper.

"Do you make a lengthy stay in London, Sir George?" he asked.

"I may stay out the Season," came the reply. "In truth, though, I find London as noisy and crowded, and full of pretensions, as I remembered from my last visit some years ago. I look forward already to returning to the simpler country life."

Forrest could hardly disagree, as Sir George mirrored his own sentiments to a great extent. Still, he doggedly tried again. "Perhaps I might be able to introduce you to some Town pleasures that are generally lacking in the country," he suggested. "One of the finer gaming establishments, for example, where the stakes are high enough to be exciting and the other, er, entertainments most delectable." If Sir George could be distracted by such amusements he would have less time for pursuing Miss Winston-Fitts, the earl reasoned.

However, Sir George declined the bait, as Lord Dearborn had somehow suspected he would. "I think not, my lord," he replied with a perfect blend of graciousness and regret. "I discovered in my youth that such pleasures are generally hollow." Though he could not be more than a year or two the earl's senior, Sir George spoke as though offering fatherly advice. "The simpler joys are more lasting, as you will no doubt find for yourself one day."

Forrest gave it up.

"I see you took me at my word that I was famished, Sir George," said Ellie as they set the loaded plates on the table. "But whatever will you yourself eat?"

This drew a general chuckle, and the slight tension that had begun to develop between the two gentlemen dissipated. Supper was a surprisingly merry meal, with Ellie and the earl trading quips, assisted in a quieter way by Sir George and even, surprisingly, by Rosalind on occasion. As a matter of fact, Forrest had to admit that he had never seen Miss Winston-Fitts so animated, though she still appeared quiet in the extreme in comparison to her more outspoken cousin. He was enjoying himself immensely, whatever the cause, and it was with some regret that he left the group to claim his next partner when the orchestra signalled the end of the supper hour.

During a lengthy recitation by Miss Adams on the trials she had endured in her quest to obtain dancing slippers of exactly the right colour to match her new ballgown, Forrest had ample time to reflect on the evening thus far. Although he had danced twice with Miss Winston-Fitts, and the second dance a waltz, he could not say that he knew any more about her than he had at the start of the evening. Indeed, he had learned more about the lovely Rosalind from her cousin, Miss O'Day, than he had from herself.

Rosalind's retiring nature was part of her charm, he reminded himself. He could never be happy with a prattler like Miss Adams, whose conversation had now progressed to the selection of the ribands for those elusive slippers. As the earl nodded politely and made some complimentary remark about her footwear, his thoughts went involuntarily to Miss O'Day. She seemed able to achieve a sort of happy medium between silence and chatter, trading barbs with ready wit or carrying on a sensible conversation without resorting to gossip or endless palaver about fashions. It was almost too bad that she was not in his style, as Miss Winston-Fitts so assuredly was.

His thoughts went again to Rosalind's greeting of Sir George Bellamy and what Miss O'Day had said about him. To be sure, there had been nothing resembling flirtation between them at the supper table, beyond the fact that Miss Winston-Fitts had shed some of her habitual shyness. Perhaps that was attributable to the fact that she simply felt more comfortable in the presence of a trusted family friend. Still, he was suddenly glad that he had not, after all, been able to obtain a third dance with her.

The music ended and Lord Dearborn, on impulse, sought out Miss O'Day for the next set. He told himself that she was probably his best source of information about Miss Winston-Fitts, though he could not deny that the prospect of matching wits with her again held a certain attraction, as well.

"Miss O'Day!" he called out, shouldering his way through the crowd of silk-and-satin-clad revellers to reach the diminutive brunette. "Might I induce you to honour me with that second dance we spoke of?"

Ellie smiled but shook her head. "I'm sorry, my lord, but my card is quite full. Perhaps at the next ball we both attend."

Forrest was conscious of an unexpected pang of disappointment. "I was right, I see. You are certainly no wallflower. Do you go to Almack's on Wednesday?"

"My aunt has not spoken of it, and I don't doubt that if she were in possession of vouchers all the world would know it." She appeared not in the least downcast at the prospect of being denied access to those exalted portals.

The earl would have prolonged his dialogue with this rather unconventional young lady had her next partner not arrived at that moment. Why could Miss

Winston-Fitts not learn her little cousin's art of conversation, he wondered irrelevantly, catching sight of Rosalind going down the dance with Viscount Strathcliffe. She was lovelier than ever, he thought, though she appeared no more at ease with the viscount than she had with himself. No, Bellamy seemed the only man outside her family with whom she was able to relax.

Lord Dearborn retired to the sidelines, contenting himself with watching Miss Winston-Fitts with her remaining partners—an enjoyable pastime. He was pleased to note that she favoured none of them with more than an occasional word or smile. By the time the evening ended, Forrest had convinced himself that the task of charming Miss Rosalind into trusting him as she did Sir George could well be a very pleasant one, indeed.

CHAPTER SIX

WHEN ELLIE AWOKE the next morning, she was astonished to discover that it was almost noon. Of course, she and the Winston-Fittses had not returned home until after three o'clock in the morning, but she could not recall ever having slept so late in her life. Bouncing out of bed, she went first to the window to revel in the brightness of the spring day. Then, reaching to pull a serviceable morning gown from the clothespress, her hand hesitated over the new riding habit. It would be a glorious day to ride in the Park, but she very much doubted that Rosalind would wish do so again today after such a late night—or even if she had been in bed by nine, for that matter. Besides, Lord Dearborn had probably completed his morning ride already.

Ellie was brought up short at the thought. Was that the real reason she wished to ride? Did she merely hope to see the earl in the Park again? Of course, he had been most obliging last night at Lady Sefton's, not only dancing with her once but actually asking her a second time. The vexation she had felt at being forced to refuse pricked at her again.

Stop it at once! she told herself sternly. Another dance would have made it only that much more difficult to subdue her growing attraction to the man, an attraction she could in no way afford to indulge. No matter that Rosalind appeared to prefer Sir George to the earl; her mother intended her to become Lady Dearborn, and Ellie had seen the results of Aunt Mabel's determination on enough other occasions to have no doubt that Lady Dearborn Rosalind would become. She herself would simply have to quell any silly longings before they became strong enough to undermine her happiness.

Determinedly, she remembered the names and faces of some of the other gentlemen she had danced with at the ball. Mr. Mulhaney had been pleasant, and quite attractive, as well, with his curling dark hair and green eyes—every bit as Irish as herself, she thought. Then there was Lord Pelton, a baron, if she remembered correctly. He had danced twice with her and flirted quite outrageously, declaring her the belle of the ball, which she had enjoyed even while she knew it to be pure gammon. And Mr. Wilshire...oh, drat it! Instead of Mr. Wilshire's thin, clever face, Lord Dearborn's bronze hair and blue eyes arose before her mind's eye.

Ellie let out her breath in exasperation. Surely it must be some perversity of her nature that made her think only of the one man she could never have. Any one of the others would be a perfectly reasonable object for a *tendre,* not to mention a better match than she had ever dared to hope for. So why in blazes couldn't she concentrate on one of them?

Without another glance at the habit, she quickly buttoned herself into the morning dress, pulled a brush through her short curls and left the room to go in search of breakfast. Not surprisingly, she was the first one downstairs, but a tempting array of ham, eggs and kippered salmon had already been laid out on the sideboard in the dining-room, so she helped herself. She was nearly finished when Rosalind entered the room, yawning widely.

"Gracious, you are up early, Ellie!" she exclaimed. "I vow, I don't know when I have been so tired as I was last night."

"No doubt you will get used to it," replied Ellie sagely. "Everyone keeps such hours in London, Lord Pelton told me."

"Mama says so also, but I far prefer country hours, I think, where breakfast is in the morning, dinner by five and bedtime well before midnight," Rosalind said decisively.

"If you become a Town hostess, you will have to change that preference, I fear," Ellie pointed out. Rosalind merely sighed and proceeded to fill a plate.

Mr. and Mrs. Winston-Fitts joined them a few minutes later, he complaining that the day was already half wasted and she full of plans for the afternoon.

"We have made an excellent start," she declared, pouring out the tea. "Peters tells me that already this morning, nearly a dozen bouquets have been delivered for Rosalind." She beamed fondly on her daughter. "Doubtless we shall be swamped with callers this afternoon, as well. It will not do, however, to rest on our laurels." She looked around the table as though daring anyone to disagree. "At five, when all the world goes to Hyde Park, you, too, must be seen there, my dear.''

Rosalind's face fell. ''Must I ride?'' she asked plaintively. ''I fear it was quite obvious to Lord Dearborn yesterday that I do not do it well.''

Mrs. Winston-Fitts regarded her for a moment, then made her decision. ''No, walking will do just as well,'' she said. ''Perhaps better, for then you may take brief rides round the Park with any eligible gentlemen that offer. It is quite an accepted practice and an excellent chance to increase any fledgling attachments.''

Ellie unwisely interrupted her aunt's battle plan at that point. ''How many attachments ought Rosalind to be encouraging, ma'am?'' she asked innocently.

Her aunt swivelled round to pierce her with a gimlet eye. ''The greater the number, the more offers she will have to choose from,'' she snapped. ''Rosalind's happiness is my first concern, as it should be yours, miss.'' Ellie successfully managed to keep her expression serious. ''Besides,'' continued Mrs. Winston-Fitts, ''if Dearborn sees that she is greatly sought after, it is like to bring him to the point all the more quickly, for fear of losing her to another.''

Ellie half expected Rosalind to voice some protest at this presumptuous ordering of her future, but her cousin remained silent. Could it be that her feelings about Lord Dearborn were beginning to change? It seemed only too likely after the attentions he had showered on her last night. Not that it would affect Ellie herself in the least, she reminded herself quickly. If Rosalind were becoming attached to the man her

mother had chosen for her, it was all to the good.
Wasn't it?

MRS. WINSTON-FITTS had been quite correct: at least
two dozen callers, more than half of them gentlemen,
descended upon them during the course of the afternoon. Lord Dearborn was not amongst them, to Ellie's mingled disappointment and relief, though he had
sent the largest bunch of flowers. She was more than
a little surprised to discover that several of the ladies,
as well as two or three of the gentlemen, seemed as
eager to make her own acquaintance as Rosalind's,
and she spent a pleasant hour making new friends. As
usual, Rosalind had little to say for herself and spent
much of her time watching the parlour door, Ellie noticed, but whether she hoped to see Lord Dearborn
walk through it or Sir George Bellamy, who was also
absent, she could not have said.

The greatest mark of distinction paid them, however, came not in the form of a caller but as a small
white envelope which was delivered just as the last one
took his leave. Mrs. Winston-Fitts plucked it from the
tray Peters offered her, but waited until she had said
her goodbyes to Mr. Whitendon to open it. Ellie was
just leaving the parlour in order to change for their
walk in the Park when she was halted by a most un-
dignified whoop from her aunt.

"Almack's!" Aunt Mabel cried, jumping up to take
Rosalind by both hands and dance her round the
room, a sight that made Ellie stare in bemusement.
"Lady Sefton must have spoken to the other patronesses. We have vouchers for Almack's! I must tell

Emmett at once!'' She ran from the room with a vigour that would have done credit to a woman half her age.

Rosalind and Ellie regarded each other rather breathlessly. Surprisingly, it was Rosalind who found her voice first.

"Mama seems extremely pleased," she said somewhat inadequately.

"I'm not surprised," replied Ellie. "The entrée to Almack's should set the final seal on your social acceptance—and hers, as well." She could well believe that Aunt Mabel saw those vouchers as a tangible trophy for all her years of work to improve her social standing.

"And yours, also, Ellie," added Rosalind. "There were four vouchers in the envelope, for I saw them."

"Were there? I—I didn't notice." Ellie's thoughts flew at once to the evening before, when Lord Dearborn had asked if she went to Almack's on Wednesday, all but promising her a dance there. Could he have had anything to do with the vouchers being sent? She reined in her errant thoughts sharply. "Well! Presuming that Aunt Mabel still wishes to walk in the Park, we'd best hurry upstairs to change," she said briskly. "Come, Rosie, let me help you with your gown."

HYDE PARK at five o'clock was thronged with those members of the fashionable world who deemed it a social necessity to assemble at that hour to see and be seen. Carriages and phaetons jostled with equestrians and pedestrians for space on the crowded paths.

Ellie looked about her with interest, taking in the panoply before them. She herself was feeling exceptionally elegant in a cambric walking dress of rose pink. The fact that the dress had belonged to Rosalind last year in no way detracted from her pleasure in it, for it became her colouring admirably and she knew it. As she observed the assortment of Society abroad in the Park, she was pleased to recognize quite a few faces, including Mrs. Millworth, whom she had met earlier that afternoon and liked quite well.

Mrs. Millworth had apparently spotted them, too, and strolled forward, along with three other ladies with whom she had been conversing. "Mrs. Winston-Fitts, Miss O' Day, Miss Winston-Fitts! How delightful to see you again so soon!" she exclaimed. "Have you met Lady Mountheath and her daughters?"

Introductions were made all round, and the seven ladies were soon in the midst of an animated discussion of fashion and gossip. Ellie quickly realized that Lady Mountheath and her daughters were especially fascinated with the latter, equipped as they were with an apparently inexhaustible supply of on dits to relate, primarily of the malicious variety. She was just deciding that she had no particular wish to become more intimate with them when Lord Dearborn drove up in a dashing royal blue high-perch phaeton.

"Give you good afternoon, ladies," he called down. "What a charming tableau you make, grouped like that. Might I prevail on you to spoil the effect somewhat by allowing Miss Winston-Fitts to take a turn about the Park with me?"

Rosalind eyed the precarious-looking vehicle with some apprehension, but her mother was already nudging her forward. "My daughter will be delighted, my lord," Mrs. Winston-Fitts said for her. "We shall go on well enough till her return, I doubt not."

Lord Dearborn's groom alighted and assisted Rosalind into the seat beside the earl. She cast one fearful glance back towards her mother and cousin before he whipped up his pair and set off at a sedate trot, threading his way between the other conveyances on the choked carriage path.

"I see that Miss Rosalind already has the elusive Lord Dearborn in her pocket," remarked Lady Mountheath waspishly as the phaeton moved away. "You are to be congratulated." Her daughters, Miss Lucy and Miss Fanny, were in their second and third Seasons respectively, and neither had yet had the luxury of refusing a single offer.

"Hardly in her pocket, my lady," replied Mrs. Winston-Fitts complacently, "but he does seem most attentive, I must admit. Perhaps you noticed last night at Lady Sefton's that he took her in to supper?"

That Lady Mountheath had was evident by the tightening of her smile. "Such a quiet, unassuming girl," she said sourly. "I have never encouraged such missishness in my own daughters, but I must say that it seems to become yours."

Mrs. Winston-Fitts was stricken momentarily speechless by this attack, but Ellie was not similarly affected. "Yes, I have noticed that Miss Fanny and Miss Lucy have no trouble expressing their opinions on any subject—or person," she said sweetly. "It is a pity that all gentlemen do not recognize the undoubted charm of such openness."

Lady Mountheath raised her lorgnette to examine this unexpected adversary. "Indeed, Miss O'Day," she said. "I have always abhorred anything akin to artifice in a young lady, to include false modesty—and cynicism."

Mrs. Millworth broke in with an animated description of some of the newest purchases for Carlton House in an obvious effort to avert any further unpleasantness, but the tension between Lady Mountheath and Miss O'Day did not noticeably abate. A few minutes later, Lord Dearborn and Rosalind completed their circuit and pulled to a halt alongside the group.

As Rosalind was handed down, Mrs. Millworth suggested that she and her original companions walk on. Lady Mountheath, however, apparently felt that her girls had been insulted and that some recompense was due them.

"I trust you had a scintillating discourse with your companion, my lord?" she asked Lord Dearborn archly. "Truly, I cannot think of another young lady with quite Miss Winston-Fitts's talent for conversation. Her wit is legendary."

Before the startled earl could reply, Ellie said wickedly, "That is doubtless because she only speaks when she has something worthwhile to say, my lady, unlike some I could name. It is the quality, rather than the quantity, of words spoken that denotes true wit."

"Well said, Miss O'Day, and I heartily agree," said Lord Dearborn before Lady Mountheath could reply. "Too many people confuse excess verbiage with intelligence, but any goose can make noise."

Lady Mountheath opened and closed her mouth several times before squawking in a strangled voice that sounded remarkably goose-like, "I shall bid you good-day then, my lord. Come, girls." Turning, she herded her daughters ahead of her, strengthening the barnyard image.

"I never did care much for that woman," remarked Lord Dearborn conversationally once she was out of earshot.

"She has the most vicious tongue I have ever heard," said Ellie heatedly. "I pray you will not regard anything she said, Rosalind."

Rosalind, who had stood as though frozen at her mother's side throughout the exchange, murmured, "Thank you, Ellie. I—I can't understand why she should dislike me so."

"It is perfectly obvious that she is motivated by jealousy," said Ellie roundly. "I can well see why, with those two hatchet-faced daughters of hers."

"Ellie!" exclaimed Rosalind, aghast, though Lord Dearborn was hard pressed to stifle a chuckle.

"Very well, I suppose I should not have said that," admitted Ellie, "but I cannot be sorry, for their tongues were very nearly as poisonous as hers. I fear I shall never develop the taste for gossip that appears to be *de rigueur* for Town life."

"That will do, Elinor," Mrs. Winston-Fitts said sharply. "I agree that Lady Mountheath was unconscionably rude, but you will not mend matters by being even more so. It is a sad truth that she is highly placed in Society and that her opinion carries some weight. We must be thankful, I suppose, that your entrée to Almack's is already assured. It is rather too late for her to turn the patronesses against you.''

''She could not if she tried,'' said Lord Dearborn knowingly. ''Sally Jersey detests the woman and would be more prone to receive someone based on her censure than on her recommendation. I must commend you, Miss O'Day, for your valiant defence of Miss Winston-Fitts. She has a staunch ally in you.'' His smile was warmer than any he had yet directed her way, and Ellie felt her heart lurch.

''Rosalind is a dear friend, as well as my cousin, my lord. I could hardly do less for her,'' she said rather breathlessly.

''I am glad to see that she has such a friend.'' He regarded her earnestly for a long moment. Then, turning abruptly to the other ladies, he said, ''Will I see you all tomorrow night at Almack's?'' At their various nods and murmurs of agreement, he added, mainly to Rosalind, ''I pray you will not be disappointed at your first sight of the rooms.'' With that enigmatic comment, he took his leave of them.

While Mrs. Millworth explained that the hall and the refreshments at Almack's were frequently disparaged by the more fastidious, Ellie gazed after Lord Dearborn's phaeton. Would he remember his half promise to dance with her? ''Staunch'' and ''valiant'' were hardly lover-like words, but he had approved of her, and that was enough . . . for now.

CHAPTER SEVEN

FORREST SLIPPED A FINGER beneath his cravat, certain that he had somehow tied it tighter than usual. This was his first visit to Almack's in two or three years, as the establishment, for all its vaunted social sanctity, was not among his favourite places to spend an evening. Of course, if he intended to shackle himself to Miss Winston-Fitts he would have to get used to this sort of thing, he told himself. Surely his constitution could manage twelve Wednesday nights out of the year of stale bread and butter and tepid lemonade for the sake of a *nonpareil* like her.

In spite of such bracing speeches to himself, the earl was beginning to waver when the Winston-Fittses arrived. However, immediately upon seeing Rosalind, resplendent in white satin overlaid with pale blue net, he felt his resolve to see it through strengthened. Miss O'Day was looking well also, he noted irrelevantly, in a canary silk gown that brought out the highlights in her dark hair. Really, it *was* almost a pity that petite brunettes were not in his style.

Moving forward, he greeted the Winston-Fittses before bowing elegantly over Rosalind's hand. "I am delighted to welcome you on your first visit to Almack's, Miss Winston-Fitts. And you, as well, Miss

O'Day. Might I prevail on each of you to honour me with an early dance?'' Rosalind looked more frightened than delighted at the prospect, and by Almack's in general, he thought, but she assented readily enough. Miss O'Day was looking about her with great interest.

"If Miss Winston-Fitts will oblige me with the first dance, dare I hope that you will reserve the second for me, Miss O'Day?'' he asked.

Ellie looked up at him with a smile. She was enjoying her first view of the celebrated Almack's immensely, in spite of its relative plainness, which she had been warned about by Mrs. Millworth. Simply being here at all was far beyond anything she had ever dreamed of, and she intended to enjoy it fully. "Certainly, my lord,'' she replied merrily to Lord Dearborn. "Dancing is what one does here, is it not?''

The earl assented that it was, for the most part. "There are a few card games to be had, but the stakes are too low to tempt the better players,'' he informed her.

"And ladies do not indulge in them?'' she asked half-seriously.

He shook his head, regarding her curiously. "Not at Almack's. Do you play at whist, by chance, Miss O'Day?''

"It has been two or three years, my lord, but I was once considered quite tolerable at it. I would be interested to discover if I retain any shred of my skill.'' She gave an exaggerated sigh. "But 'twill have to be another time, I apprehend.''

"None of the Winston-Fittses play?" he asked, glancing back to Rosalind, who stood listening to their banter in silence. She shook her head as Ellie responded.

"No, my aunt has an aversion to cards and so has never encouraged Rosie to learn. My uncle may possibly play, but never at home, I assure you!" She glanced quickly over her shoulder to ascertain that Aunt Mabel was not attending.

Lord Dearborn chuckled. "Well, it is to be hoped that you receive an opportunity to revive your skills in the near future, Miss O'Day. Miss Winston-Fitts, I shall return for you when the orchestra signals the first set." Bowing, he wandered off to pay his respects to those patronesses whom he had not yet encountered since the start of the Season.

Rosalind had been surreptitiously watching the door during the earl's conversation with her cousin. Several of her erstwhile admirers were arriving, to her mother's gratification, if not her own. After Lord Dearborn moved off, she turned to Ellie.

"He seemed very kind, don't you think?" she asked. "You were right, Ellie, that Lord Dearborn is most handsome. Do you not look forward to your dance with him?"

Ellie did not notice Rosalind's uncharacteristically sly expression, which might have warned her that her cousin was hatching some sort of plan. Instead, Ellie's heart sank at her cousin's praise of the earl. It appeared that she was not immune to his charms, after all!

"Certainly, Rosie," she managed to reply. "But do not forget that it was you he engaged for the first set. Surely that is a signal honour, and one he has paid you before."

Rosalind smiled enigmatically. "Yes, I suppose so. Look, here come Mr. Wilshire and Lord Gresham." Private conversation was impossible after that, for Rosalind was surrounded by her usual throng of eager beaux and forced to pay shy attention to each. Ellie was similarly besieged by admirers, though not in such great numbers. By the time the first strains of music sounded, both young ladies were engaged for the first several sets.

"Miss Winston-Fitts, my dance, I believe." Lord Dearborn appeared as though by magic, skilfully extricating Rosalind from the crowd about her.

Ellie, on the arm of Lord Pelton, followed them onto the floor to take her place for the opening minuet. Lord Pelton flirted with her at every opportunity during the old-fashioned dance, but Ellie's attention kept wandering farther down the set to where Rosalind and Lord Dearborn were dancing.

Was her cousin finally softening towards him? she wondered. Her earlier remark certainly had implied that. Ellie had little doubt that if Rosalind were to show herself receptive to the earl's attentions he would offer for her without delay. She suspected that it was only an admirable reluctance to press his suit in the face of her apparent indifference that had prevented him from doing so already. He must know that Rosalind would not be permitted to refuse him, and would not wish to force her to an unwelcome match.

Ellie steadfastly ignored the heaviness that had descended on her heart and smiled brilliantly up at Lord Pelton in response to his next outrageous compliment. He *was* a baron, after all, and she could scarcely afford to whistle such a suitor down the wind in her present situation, even if he was well past forty. Despite her brave words to Rosalind last week, Ellie was by no means certain that she would have the option of living in Ireland after her cousin's wedding, and even a loveless marriage would surely be preferable to living indefinitely on sufferance in her aunt's household.

In spite of herself, Ellie's spirits lightened when Lord Dearborn claimed her for the next dance. He was amusing to talk to, even if he could never care for her in the way she was finally admitting to herself that she cared for him. To her surprise, the orchestra struck up the strains of a waltz as she took his arm.

"Oh, dear," she said, suppressing a surge of disappointment. "Do not the patronesses have to give permission before I may waltz here?" Lady Sefton was the only patroness she was at all acquainted with, and she had not noticed whether she were even present tonight.

"Indeed they do, and the Countess Lieven and Lady Jersey were kind enough to do so after I requested to be allowed to dance it with you," he replied imperturbably. "I quite enjoyed our waltz at Lady Sefton's, and desired to repeat the experience."

"How...how did you know that this would be a waltz?" she asked curiously. Mrs. Millworth had told her that every ball at Almack's began with a minuet, but she had not thought that the other dances were so ordered.

"I have certain, ah, connections," answered the earl with a twinkle. "Shall we, Miss O'Day?"

Since he had apparently thought of everything, Ellie went willingly into his light clasp for the dance that some still considered mildly scandalous, her errant heart beating a giddy tattoo. He had requested the waltz so that he could dance it with her? It seemed unbelievable in the extreme, but no doubt he had his reasons.

"Does Sir George Bellamy not have the entrée here, Miss O'Day?" he asked.

So! He wished to waltz with her so that he could question her further about Rosalind's friendship with Sir George, she thought. The mystery was solved, not entirely to her satisfaction. "I do not know, my lord, but I would doubt it."

"Why?" he asked.

"Because he is not here," she replied simply.

Lord Dearborn chuckled. "A most logical young lady, I see. No doubt that quality serves you well at whist."

"I like to think so," she returned with a smile. "Tell me, my lord, do you play? You seem inordinately interested in my level of skill but have revealed nothing about your own. I suspect you are no novice at it yourself."

"I am found out!" he said in mock despair. "I had hoped to engage you in a game for outrageously high stakes and win quite a fortune before you discovered that."

Ellie had to laugh. "I am not so green as that, my lord. Nor would I gamble more than I can afford to lose, so I fear that the stakes would be a sore disappointment to a gentleman like yourself—on the order of a penny or two." She spoke lightly, not stopping to consider that her extreme poverty could hardly be considered an asset.

Forrest noted what her words revealed, but was chiefly struck by her utter lack of embarrassment as she admitted to it. When he had referred to her as "valiant" yesterday, he had seemingly been more right than he knew. Miss O'Day obviously faced an uncertain future, but she did so cheerfully, with both eyes open. Courage was a quality Forrest had always admired, wherever he saw it, and his respect for this young woman rose even higher.

He had just boasted of having a certain amount of influence, he reflected. Perhaps he could use it to benefit Miss O'Day. The earl had never been one to play the matchmaker, but he could not help but think that a good marriage might be just the thing for a girl of her mettle. Mentally, he went over some of the eligible bachelors he knew, but found none that met the standards he felt such a sprightly, intelligent girl deserved. Clearly, this plan would require more thought.

"A skilful player may parlay a penny or two into pounds, I have found," he said with a smile. "I look forward to facing you across the cards, Miss O'Day, even if the stakes are imaginary." To his surprise, he found that he meant it.

Though Forrest's original intent in engaging Miss O'Day for a waltz had been to discover more of Miss

Winston-Fitts through her, the dance somehow ended without her name ever arising between them. Curiously, he did not realize it until long afterwards, when he was again dancing with the beauteous Rosalind.

"Your cousin is very amusing," he commented, breaking their customary silence.

Rosalind smiled, a breathtaking sight. "Oh, yes! Ellie is quite the cleverest girl I have ever known," she agreed at once.

"She seems remarkably content with her lot in life," he hazarded.

"Oh, Ellie is almost never blue-devilled, whatever demands my mother makes upon her," Rosalind informed him. "I believe she could be happy working as a scullery maid."

Forrest quite failed to notice that Miss Winston-Fitts had just favoured him with more words together than she had ever done before. Instead, he was struggling with the disturbing picture of Miss O'Day toiling as a servant to the autocratic Mrs. Winston-Fitts.

"Surely she has prospects open to her?" he asked.

"She has made some mention of removing to her grandfather in Ireland," said Rosalind. "I have tried to convince her that she would be happier married, but she seems to think that unlikely, though Lord Pelton has been quite attentive."

The earl missed the speculative look Rosalind directed at him as she shared this bit of news. The thought of Miss O'Day in Ireland cheered him no more than that of her married to Lord Pelton, a man whose reputation made his own appear pristine by comparison. "Pray do not press her to encourage his

suit, Miss Winston-Fitts,'' he finally said. "I am persuaded that a young lady of Miss O'Day's capabili-
ties can do better.''

Rosalind said no more, well satisfied with the progress of her plan.

On the far side of the room, Ellie was sitting out her
first dance of the evening, grateful for the chance to
catch her breath. She was finding it more difficult tonight to convince herself that the gentlemen who had
danced with her did so only because they could not
engage Rosalind. Indeed, at least two or three had
asked her first. While she was gratified by her apparent success, a feeling of incompleteness, of something
not quite right, marred her usual cheerfulness. Gazing out across the room from her chair near the wall,
she caught sight of Rosalind waltzing with Lord
Dearborn and her vague discontent suddenly took on
a recognizable form.

Jealous? Am I actually jealous of Rosalind? The
idea was distasteful in the extreme. Surely, she loved
her cousin and only wanted what was best for her. But
there it was. Seeing Rosalind with Lord Dearborn, she
felt a welling of unpleasant emotion that could only
signal the advent of that hateful, green-ey'd monster,
as Shakespeare had named it. Unhappily, she watched
the two of them moving about the floor and realized
with a fresh pang that Rosalind was actually speaking
to the earl, showing far more animation than had
previously been her wont with him.

Silently, Ellie chided herself fiercely for her foolish
infatuation with someone as unattainable to one in her
circumstances as the Earl of Dearborn. He was en-

joyable to be with, of course, but that was no excuse
for her silliness of fancying herself in love with the
man. Perhaps, if she could stifle her inappropriate
feelings for him, they could at least be friends. Yes,
that would surely be her best course—the only one that
might offer her any peace of mind, any future happiness at all. For it was increasingly apparent that Rosalind was beginning to return his regard, and that
their marriage could not be far distant.

She nodded determinedly to herself, and when Mr.
Mulhaney stepped up a moment later to claim her for
the next dance, she favoured him with a brilliant smile.
Ellie refused to allow any ridiculous infatuation to
spoil her first visit to Almack's, or her one London
Season!

"WHEN ARE WE TO HEAR the happy announcement?" asked Lady Jersey of Lord Dearborn as the
evening drew near to a close. "It must be a powerful
inducement that has brought you back to us after so
long an absence, and I believe I can guess what it is."
She waggled her eyebrows suggestively at him and
nodded in the direction of the entrance, where the
Winston-Fittses were waiting for their carriage.

Forrest smiled. He knew that Sally Jersey's tongue
could be acerbic when she chose, but he had never
been on the sharp end of it himself and held her in
some affection, as did his mother. "Miss Winston-
Fitts is undeniably lovely," he admitted, "and I'll not
deny she comes closer to my ideal than any lady I've
met for the past six or seven Seasons."

"Which is all you've spent in London," rejoined Lady Jersey, nodding wisely. "Of course, there is more to an enduring match than a pretty face, but I'm sure you are aware of that. Doubtless the young lady has additional charms to recommend her?"

"Indubitably." She was blatantly fishing for more information, but Forrest deflected her question with one of his own. "What do you know of the cousin, Miss O'Day? I presume you discovered something of her background before inviting her here." If he was to help the girl, he must know a little bit about her, he told himself.

"Yes, isn't she a treasure?" Lady Jersey exclaimed, momentarily diverted. "She has quite taken the gentlemen by storm, though I doubt that she realizes it yet. Her humour and wit more than make up for her lack of the more obvious sort of beauty. And her family is positively ancient! Winston-Fitts through her mother, of course—quite a toast twenty or so years back, Maria Sefton tells me. And her father was Lord Kerrigan's second son, one of the oldest Irish titles. It is a pity she has not the fortune to complement such impeccable bloodlines." Lady Jersey was waxing eloquent, and Forrest had no particular desire to stop the flow.

"I daresay she will make a creditable match even without it," she continued. "The more thoughtful gentlemen are already commenting on her cleverness and cheerful disposition, traits not to be despised in a wife, surely."

"Indeed not," agreed the earl. "Do you mention any gentleman in particular?" He found himself hoping it would not be Pelton.

Lady Jersey shot him a penetrating glance. "Mr. Mulhaney has made no secret of his admiration, but of course he hasn't a feather to fly with and cannot afford to marry where there is no money. I noticed also that both Lord Pelton and Sir Martin Coates danced twice with her, and neither of them needs to marry a fortune. I daresay she will have many suitors to choose among—nearly as many as the dazzling Miss Winston-Fitts."

"Thank you, ma'am," said Forrest. While it was what he had hoped to hear, her disclosures did not give him the satisfaction he had expected. "Since my future is likely to include Miss Winston-Fitts, I thought it would behoove me to discover what I could of her connections. She appears to hold Miss O'Day in great affection. I had thought to do something for the girl, to please Miss Winston-Fitts, but from what you say it may prove unnecessary. I appreciate your candour." Bowing, he took his leave.

Lady Jersey watched him speculatively as he made his way to the door. She did not doubt for a moment that Lord Dearborn might be able to do something for Miss O'Day—perhaps far more than he intended at present. For now, however, she would keep her own counsel. The earl was quite a favourite of hers, and not even for the sake of being first with so extraordinary an on dit would she jeopardize his future happiness with an untimely word.

CHAPTER EIGHT

MABEL WINSTON-FITTS looked about her in satisfaction. All was in readiness for her dinner party, Rosalind's formal introduction to Society. The flowers were delivered and arranged, the parlour polished and dusted to a fare-thee-well, and the dining table set for twenty-four with the best china and crystal. What did it matter that her daughter's debut was not to be a ball? After two balls in three days, she had convinced herself that a more intimate grouping was far preferable and more conducive to prompting a certain gentleman to declare his feelings for Rosalind.

That he was intending to do so she could no longer doubt. Why, that very day she had received an invitation from his mother, the Countess of Dearborn, for the family to attend a house party at his estate. Surely that indicated a desire to introduce his intended to his mother as well as to give Rosalind, and her parents, a glimpse of her future home! Yes, Mrs. Winston-Fitts was in very high spirits, indeed.

"We are dressed, Mama. Is there anything you wish us to do?" Rosalind asked as she and Ellie descended from their bedchambers.

"Just be your lovely self, my angel," replied Mrs. Winston-Fitts, turning to regard her daughter fondly.

Rosalind looked superb in her new evening gown of silvery-white sarsenet. Her golden hair was piled high on her head and interwoven with tiny white orchids, making her look like a virgin goddess.

Mrs. Winston-Fitts's smile faded slightly as she turned to inspect her niece. That lilac silk was to have been Rosalind's, but when they had received the vouchers to Almack's, Elinor had come up one dress short. Unwilling to have even a poor relation disgrace them at that hallowed establishment, she had directed her niece to wear Rosalind's yellow silk, necessitating hurried instructions to the dressmaker to have this lilac one made to fit Elinor's dimensions rather than Rosalind's. With her shining dark curls gathered into a loose, fashionable knot on the top of her head, she looked more attractive than her aunt would have thought possible for such a little dab of a thing.

"You'll do, Elinor," she finally said, earning a startled glance from her niece at the unexpected praise. "Pray try to comport yourself with dignity, and refrain from fidgeting or bouncing about. And speak as little as possible—this is to be Rosalind's night, remember."

Ellie nodded obediently. "I shall do my best, Aunt Mabel," she said. Truly, she had not the smallest wish to detract from Rosalind's début.

"I have noticed one or two gentlemen paying you marked attentions," continued her aunt. "Lord Pelton will be amongst the guests, and I have seated you by him. Mind everything I've told you and you may be lucky enough to receive an offer." Her smile soured, as though she found the thought of her niece as a baroness somehow distasteful.

Ellie tried to show a proper enthusiasm at the prospect. At least as Lady Pelton she would no longer be subject to Aunt Mabel's whims. "I'll be everything that is proper, ma'am," she promised with tolerable cheerfulness.

"I take leave to doubt that, but I do hope you will try. Ah, Emmett, here you are at last! Let us go down to the front door at once. Our guests will be arriving at any moment."

"You look very fetching tonight, Ellie," her uncle informed her in an undertone before descending. "Our little dark horse may yet win the race this Season." Leaving Ellie to ponder the meaning of that remark, he followed his wife to the ground floor.

"LORD DEARBORN, do try this turbot—it is Cook's specialty," cooed Mrs. Winston-Fitts to the earl, who was seated on her right. "And will you not have a bit more breast of veal?" She motioned to the footman to bring the platter back to that end of the long table.

"Thank you, no, ma'am," responded Lord Dearborn, negating her order to the footman with a quick shake of his head. "I am endeavouring to ration my appetite that I shall be able to partake of every delicacy you offer." He turned to smile meaningfully at Miss Winston-Fitts on his other side as he spoke.

Rosalind kept her eyes on her plate, but her mother seized upon the compliment at once with a trilling laugh. "Oh, la! How clever, my lord. Of course, nothing I have planned for the table can match my daughter, but you are wise not to stuff yourself just yet. There are still two more courses, with three or four removes to each. I dare swear our Cook is amongst the finest in London, though temperamental as all these Frenchmen are." She spoke proudly, and at sufficient volume for the majority of her guests to hear.

Forrest smiled politely and murmured another pleasantry about the food before turning back to Rosalind. "Have I mentioned how lovely you are looking tonight, Miss Winston-Fitts?" he asked, though he clearly recalled complimenting her on her appearance when he had arrived. His only choice, however, was between conversing with her or her mother, and this seemed as good an opening remark as any.

"Yes, thank you, my lord," she replied, not quite meeting his gaze. Forrest saw with regret that her unwonted volubility of the night before had apparently subsided already.

"Have you been to the theatre yet?" he then asked, still unwilling to submit himself to his other dinner partner's discourse.

"Not yet, my lord. We go next week."

"Ah. I have no doubt you will enjoy it immensely." *For it will require no conversation whatsoever,* he added silently.

Instantly berating himself for the disloyal thought, he tried the subject that had spurred her last night to become more communicative. "I see your mother has placed Miss O'Day next to Lord Pelton. Is she trying for a match there, do you think?" He kept his voice low, though it was unlikely that his hostess, enthusi-astically extolling the virtues of the stewed eels to Lord Ellerby on her left, would overhear him.

Rosalind followed his glance to where Ellie sat near the middle of the table, between Lord Pelton and Sir George Bellamy. "My mother may wish it, but I think Ellie may favour someone else," she confided, look-ing sidelong at him.

Forrest missed the look, watching Miss O'Day as she spoke animatedly to Sir George. Something she said made him laugh, and the earl frowned. Could it be the squire that she preferred? Perhaps he had mis-read the signals and it was Miss O'Day rather than Miss Winston-Fitts who held more than a friendly af-fection for Sir George. Certainly, the man seemed to treat her with exceptional kindness. No doubt that would be an admirable solution to two different problems, he thought discontentedly.

"I am glad to see that she is not encouraging Pel-ton, at any rate," he remarked, wondering why he was not more pleased at the thought of a match between Miss O'Day and Sir George. "The man has a rather unsavoury reputation, I am afraid."

"Oh! I . . . I shall warn her of it, my lord," assured Rosalind, with a half smile at this promising show of concern.

"That might be wise," he agreed, turning his full attention back to his intended. What a bewitching smile Miss Winston-Fitts had!

"Lord Dearborn, it was vastly obliging of your mama to invite us to her house party," broke in Mrs. Winston-Fitts at that moment, in a voice that could doubtless be heard in the kitchens. "I vow, I am quite agog at the prospect of seeing your estate. Huntington Park it is called, is it not?"

He assented that it was, and was subjected to a lengthy treatise on what his hostess had been able to discover about his ancestral home for the remainder of the first course and most of the second.

When the ladies adjourned to the drawing-room, leaving the gentlemen to their port, Rosalind went at once to Ellie's side. "I had a rather enlightening conversation with Lord Dearborn," she said conspiratorially. Involuntarily, Ellie winced at her words. Rosalind appeared startled by her reaction and Ellie endeavoured to cover her distress with a smile.

"That is wonderful, Rosie," she said so cheerfully that Rosalind's face cleared at once. "I am so pleased that you and he seem able to converse comfortably now. If you can once bring yourself to be easy in his presence, I have no doubt that the two of you will go on famously together." At that point, they were joined by Mrs. Millworth and Lady Ellerby, a pretty young matron with hair of the same bright gold as Rosalind's and the conversation perforce turned to more general topics.

Ellie was determinedly merry for the remainder of the evening, exchanging quips with her aunt's guests or listening sympathetically to whatever tales of scandal or woe they cared to share. Never before, however, had she had to work so hard at the gaiety that normally came so naturally to her. She kept reminding herself that if she loved Rosalind as a cousin and Lord Dearborn as a friend, she should in truth feel the happiness she was trying so diligently to project, and by the time the gentlemen joined them she had almost managed to convince herself that she did.

Thus, she was able to smile brightly when the earl approached her, her cousin's name the first words out of his mouth. "Miss Winston-Fitts tells me you all go to the theatre next week," he said. "Will Sir George perchance be a member of your party?"

Ellie clung valiantly to her smile. Couldn't the man speak of anything else? Surely he must see that he had no cause whatsoever to be jealous of poor Sir George! "I am not certain, my lord," she replied. "My aunt has not mentioned it to me."

"Ah! Perhaps I shall mention it to her, then," he said with a wink and promptly went in search of his hostess.

That tactic seemed to smack of playing foul, Ellie thought, which she would not have expected of him. Of course Sir George would not be invited if Lord Dearborn specifically requested otherwise! No doubt Aunt Mabel would extend an invitation to the earl instead, which would ensure at least one more trying evening of watching him flirt with Rosalind.

But no, she was *happy* for Rosalind, she reminded herself quickly, and should welcome such solicitude on the part of her most eligible suitor. Pinning the corners of her mouth back up, Ellie went across to join a lively debate between her uncle and Mr. Carruthers, a prominent member of Parliament, on the relative merits of the Corn Laws and soon forgot her conflicting emotions in heated political discourse.

"Your niece appears to be a girl of many parts," commented Mrs. Carruthers to her hostess a short while later. "I declare, it is so refreshing to hear a young lady express her opinions on something besides the current fashions! Though, of course, she seems well able to hold her own on that topic, as well."

"Oh, er, yes," said Mrs. Winston-Fitts, glancing around to where Ellie was now surrounded by the younger members of the party, many of whom were laughing quite immoderately. "Elinor is quite clever."

"Indeed she is, but no bluestocking for all that," agreed Mrs. Carruthers warmly. "You must be extremely proud of her, ma'am. Everyone is saying what a delight Miss O'Day is, and what an asset she is to any gathering. Hostesses will be clamouring after her, I don't doubt. Oh, you must excuse me. She is about to tell the story of the addle-pated cow, and I so wish to hear it!" She hurried away to join the group around Ellie.

Mabel Winston-Fitts thoughtfully watched her go, a slight frown marring her brow. It appeared that Elinor was again in danger of eclipsing Rosalind, in spite of all her strictures. She would have to take her aside for another talk, it would seem.

ELLIE WAS ENJOYING her first visit to Covent Garden far more than she had expected to. The audience was nearly as diverting as the play, making it quite obvious that more of them had come to be seen than to watch the scheduled entertainment. However, *As You Like It* was one of her favourites, and once the curtain rose she had little attention to spare for the strutting dandies or elegantly clad occupants of the boxes. Neither Edmund Kean nor Sarah Siddons were members of the cast, to her regret, but the actors were still far superior to those she had witnessed in the few country theatricals she had attended.

Seated between Lord Dearborn and Sir George Bellamy, she found it disconcertingly easy to pretend that the earl was her escort rather than Rosalind's. Indeed, it seemed that he directed more comments on the performance to her than to her cousin, but that was likely because she had admitted earlier to being a great admirer of Shakespeare. Ellie rather doubted that Rosalind had ever read a single one of the Bard's plays, even this one that boasted her namesake.

"Watch this fellow playing the old Duke," whispered Lord Dearborn, leaning towards her again. "I saw him last autumn in *A Midsummer Night's Dream*, as Egeus. He was quite good."

Ellie had to agree the man was excellent. It was a shame he was too old to play most of the leading roles. By the time the play ended, she felt that her understanding of Shakespeare, already well above the average, had been much elevated by the earl's informed commentary. How pleasant it would be to always have such a companion.

Abruptly, she caught herself up. As a friend, of course, only as a friend! She was quite resigned by this time that Lord Dearborn could never be more to her than that.

"A very good performance, do you not agree, Miss O'Day?" asked Sir George as the lights came up.

Ellie agreed wholeheartedly, wondering again why Aunt Mabel had included him in the party. Mrs. Winston-Fitts had by no means been encouraging Sir George before now, and besides, had not Lord Dearborn asked that he be excluded? It seemed inconceivable that her aunt might have disregarded any request of the earl's, however, so he must not have done so, after all. Ellie wondered suddenly if Lord Dearborn could be promoting a match between herself and Sir George to safeguard Rosalind from him. At the thought, she had to stifle a giggle, so that when she turned back to Lord Dearborn at his next remark her eyes were still dancing.

"What did you say, my lord?"

"I was merely asking whether you enjoyed the play, but I can see that you did. It is a rare young lady who properly appreciates Shakespeare's humour today."

Since she could obviously not reveal the true cause of her mirth, Ellie made no effort to correct him. Besides, she *had* enjoyed the play enormously. And she was certain—well, almost certain—that she would have enjoyed it just as much had the earl not been present.

THE NEXT FEW WEEKS of the Season went by in a veritable blur of balls, routs, excursions and tea parties. Ellie considered herself very fortunate to be Rosalind's companion, invited everywhere with her beautiful cousin. Little did she suspect that she herself was the principal cause for most of the invitations, and that Rosalind was the addendum. Mrs. Carruthers had been quite correct in her prediction that hostesses would consider the lively, clever Miss O'Day a desirable addition to their entertainments.

Mrs. Winston-Fitts had finally given up trying to stifle her irrepressible niece, for she had reluctantly realized what Elinor seemed unaware of: that she was a social asset to the entire family. That knowledge rankled, for she would far have preferred her own daughter to be the one so sought after, but she was not so mean-spirited as to punish Elinor for what she could not help. Nor was she above taking full advantage of her niece's popularity.

The gentlemen, at least, still seemed to prefer Rosalind over her unremarkable little cousin, though Elinor *could* boast of two or three improbably high-ranking suitors. Among Rosalind's admirers, Lord Dearborn was still the most persistent, though Mrs. Winston-Fitts was growing increasingly frustrated by his reluctance to come to the point. True, there were at least three others, equally wealthy if not so highly titled, who would be perfectly acceptable sons-in-law, but she had her heart set on seeing her daughter a countess.

The problem was, Rosalind still was making not the slightest push to attach Lord Dearborn—or anyone else—as a husband. True, Rosalind would doubtless accept that bucolic squire, Sir George, were he to offer, but her mother had taken some pains to be certain the opportunity could not occur. Whenever he had called, she herself had received him, and with such frigid politeness that he generally left before Rosalind knew he had arrived. His calls had been much less frequent of late.

As for Rosalind, Mrs. Winston-Fitts was becoming quite exasperated with her. She began to fear that it might even be possible, albeit barely, for her daughter to finish out the Season unbetrothed!—no, no, that was unthinkable. In all likelihood, Lord Dearborn was simply waiting for the more romantic setting of the house party to make her an offer. He would be leaving for the country in a day or two, he had said. Of course, there was still Lady Allbeck's rout tonight. Perhaps, with some adroit manoeuvring, something might be contrived there. Not yet would she give up her hopes of seeing Rosalind a countess!

CHAPTER NINE

ELLIE CAUGHT HER BREATH in delight as the coach rounded the high brick wall to pass through open wrought-iron gates, affording the party their first glimpse of Huntington Park. The gravelled drive wound for nearly a quarter of a mile through manicured emerald lawns dotted with daisies and graced by towering oaks and flowering fruit trees, ending in a broad sweep before the loveliest house she had ever seen. Of mellow stone, the original Tudor block of the main house had apparently been added to over the past three centuries according to the taste of the successive owners, resulting in a curious, but charming, blend of architectural styles. To Ellie, the graceful columns, towers and domes, the mullioned windows twinkling in the sunlight, gave the house an almost fairy-tale appearance.

"Gracious!" cried Mrs. Winston-Fitts on seeing the rambling mansion. "Rosalind, when you become mistress here, you simply *must* prevail upon Lord Dearborn to have this monstrosity torn down and replaced by a proper modern house. I vow, this place could give one nightmares!"

"Aunt Mabel, how can you say so?" exclaimed Ellie in surprise. "I think it absolutely beautiful!" Ignoring her aunt's quelling glance, she turned to her cousin. "Surely you wouldn't wish to destroy all this history simply to have a house like everyone else's, Rosie?"

Rosalind only murmured noncommittally that the house looked very pretty to her as it was.

Ellie thought that Rosalind had been unusually quiet, even for her, during the six-hour drive from London, and she wondered at it. One would have thought that she would be the happiest of women after Lord Dearborn's near-declaration on his last night in Town. That evening, at a rout at Lady Allbeck's, he had danced three times with Miss Winston-Fitts, and her mother, at least, had been in raptures ever since. Ellie privately marvelled that she had not had an announcement put in the papers immediately.

She herself had enjoyed two dances with the earl, the second being the last of the evening. Ellie felt that she was progressing nicely in her plan to relegate her feelings for Lord Dearborn to the realm of mere friendship. During both their dances, they had teased each other and spoken on numerous topics of general interest, discovering much in common, but not one lover-like glance or phrase had occurred on either side. Of course, she had never expected such from *him,* but she congratulated herself that *she* had betrayed no hint of her infatuation to either the earl or any onlookers. It would never do for Rosalind to guess the truth!

Rosalind, however, had appeared to share none of her mother's delight at the singular compliment Lord Dearborn had paid her with that third dance. Really, it made Ellie wonder whether her cousin were not indifferent to the man after all—but of course if she were, she would never have consented to that fateful dance, which was tantamount to a public declaration of his intentions.

To distract herself from these less than gratifying recollections, Ellie gave her attention to the pastoral delights outside the carriage window. A shallow, pebbly stream ran alongside the drive for some way before turning across their path, at which point a charming blue-and-white bridge spanned the sparkling water. Ellie could not help but smile at the sight of a graceful mother swan, with nine little cygnets in tow, paddling towards them along the little brook.

Suddenly, they were there. The carriage halted before the imposing columned portico, and a footman leapt down to open the door and lower the steps. Breathing deeply of the fresh country air, Ellie followed the Winston-Fittses out onto the drive.

"I—I had no idea Huntington Park would be so *big*," said Rosalind, looking about her in awe.

"Yes, my dear, think how grand that you will soon be mistress of it all," said her mother complacently, taking in the view of the lawns with a proprietary air. "Not that you will spend as much time here as in London, of course."

Ellie thought Rosalind looked more than a little frightened at the prospect and sought to soothe her. "Don't worry, dear. I don't doubt Lord Dearborn has an army of servants, under a very able housekeeper, to deal with all of the day-to-day workings of the place. And of course, there is his mother, the countess."

As if on cue, the front door opened, and the earl and his mother stood there to greet them. Lord Dearborn looked incredibly handsome in his dark blue riding coat and gleaming boots, but it was the countess who drew all eyes. Swathed in violet and crimson silk, she wore rubies and amethysts at her throat, wrists and ears, while red and purple feathers swayed above her high-piled white hair, giving an impression of regal height to her diminutive frame.

"Welcome, welcome, Mr. and Mrs. Winston-Fitts!" she cried, coming forward with hands outstretched. "And *this* must be Rosalind!" She paused briefly to survey her son's chosen lady with apparent delight before turning to Ellie.

"My niece, Miss O'Day," supplied Mr. Winston-Fitts when his wife made no move to present her.

"Of course. Welcome, dear. Please, won't you all come inside? Hutchins will show you to your rooms, and you can rest and freshen up after your journey before joining us in the main parlour. Only two or three others have yet arrived, but I expect several more within the hour, as the weather is so fine. Indeed, we should have a delightful summer, as the oak was in leaf well before the ash this spring."

They all advanced into the vaulted front hall while she spoke, and when his mother paused for breath, Forrest took the opportunity to greet his guests. "Your presence enhances my home, Miss Winston-Fitts," he said to Rosalind after exchanging pleasantries with her parents and Miss O'Day. "I hope you will be most comfortable here. If you should want for anything, you need only ask."

Rosalind avoided his eye during this speech, but Mrs. Winston-Fitts preened at the obvious implication that her daughter was to regard Huntington Park as her home. "You are most gracious, my lord," she fairly twittered before Rosalind's silence could become noticeable. "I was just telling the others as we came up the drive that I have never seen such a lovely house in my life. I have no doubt that Rosalind will find everything perfectly to her liking, as shall we."

On that cordial note, the newly arrived guests repaired to the chambers prepared for them, taking interested notice of their surroundings as they went. Ellie thought the entry hall simply magnificent with its domed ceiling and marble floor of white and gold. The great staircase mounted to a sort of balcony, which ran along three sides at the first floor level, the numerous arches off it no doubt leading to various living chambers. It was all far grander than anything she had ever seen, quite eclipsing her grandfather's great house at Kerribrooke. Oddly, though, rather than being intimidated by such grandeur, she felt somehow at home—as though she belonged here.

Don't you only wish! she chided herself as they mounted the curving staircase at the rear of the enormous hall, which surely did duty as a ballroom at times. Still, she could not completely dispel the comforting feeling that she had come home at last.

The feeling intensified when she was shown into the lovely bedchamber she was to occupy for the duration of the house party. Having peeked into Rosalind's room when the portly butler opened the door for her, intoning, "The Gold Room," she understood that most of the guest rooms must have such colour "themes." Rosalind's had been draped, carpeted and furnished in shades of gold, while hers was done in various shades of pink.

"What is this room called, pray?" she impulsively asked Hutchins as he turned away.

"The Rose Room," he replied imperturbably.

"It's beautiful. Thank you," she said. He merely bowed in response, but she thought she detected a slight softening in the rigid lines around his mouth.

Advancing into the room, she realized that the name was even more appropriate than she had first thought. Not only were the carpet, curtains and wallpaper rose coloured, but all had roses worked into their designs, as well. It would be easy to pretend one was nestled in the heart of a rose bower here, she thought. Suddenly, it occurred to her to wonder who had assigned her this room. Could Lord Dearborn have done it? She vaguely recalled mentioning an affinity for flowers, and for roses in particular, to him during their last dance together. More likely, though, the countess, or even the housekeeper, had been responsible for the allocation of guest rooms, she supposed. Whoever it had been, whether by design or not, she was grateful. It was a room she could feel comfortable in—a sanctuary.

As the day was warm and she was no longer in chilly, formal London, Ellie impulsively decided to change into one of the few dresses she had brought with her to the Winston-Fittses' and that her Aunt Mabel had been willing to let her keep. Her ice-blue flowered calico seemed perfect for a summer house party. It had always been one of her favourites and it fit her to perfection, even if it were not in the first stare of fashion. Her heart lighter than it had been in weeks—perhaps months—Ellie left her lovely room to discover whether the Winston-Fittses were ready to join the party.

Rosalind opened at once to her tap, forestalling the abigail who was still fussing with her hair.

"That will do, Simms, thank you," she said mildly, dismissing the woman. "Ellie, you look so cool and fresh! Why have I not seen that gown before?"

"Oh, it's just an old one I had from...before. I would never have dared wear it in Town, nor would Aunt Mabel have allowed me to, I am certain. How do you like your room?" Preferring not to talk about herself, Ellie turned to examine the shimmering golden carpets, curtains and furnishings that adorned Rosalind's chamber. Though it was not nearly as cosy and welcoming as her own, its size and aspect indicated that it was likely the best guest room.

"It's...it's very nice," admitted Rosalind with a surprising lack of enthusiasm. "I'm sure it was very kind of Lord Dearborn to let me have it." She glanced about her with a wistful smile.

"What's wrong, my dear?" asked Ellie quickly. "Are you having second thoughts about marrying him?"

Rosalind's head came up. "Second thoughts? I never had first ones! Besides, he has not yet offered for me, though you and Mama keep talking as though he had. Perhaps he has no intention of doing so! But there, I'm sorry I snapped at you, Ellie. Let us go and see if Mama and Papa are ready to go down.'' She snatched up her gloves and preceded her startled cousin out of the room.

Mrs. Winston-Fitts grimaced when she saw Ellie's gown but said nothing, merely bidding her husband to make haste. By the time the group reached the ground floor, Ellie thought she had figured out the reason for Rosalind's uncharacteristic outburst a few minutes earlier. No doubt she was fearing that the earl did not intend to propose, after all, which would surely account for an unsettled state of mind, especially if Rosalind loved him. And how could she not? Ellie did not believe for an instant that Rosie had any cause for worry, but she could certainly sympathize with her feelings—all too well, in fact!

They were directed to the main parlour by a footman, though the hum of voices emanating from the room would have shown them their way just as well. The large, beautifully appointed room opened directly off the great hall and echoed it in elegance, if not quite in size. The countess rose to greet them upon their entry, much as she had when they first arrived, her face wreathed in smiles of apparently genuine delight.

"Ah, here you are! See, Forrest, the Winston-Fittses were not so tired. I told you they would not be, after such a short drive on so fine a day! Let me present the others here to you. This is Sir William and Lady Fenwick, who live in the neighbourhood and who are dear friends." She indicated an enormously fat gentleman, who had struggled to his feet with no little effort and now swept them a surprisingly graceful bow. His wife, also of ample proportions, smiled and greeted them most graciously. Ellie felt herself warming to them at once.

The countess continued, "This is my daughter Juliet, Lady Glenhaven, and her husband, Lord Glenhaven. Come, Teddy, you needn't be so stiff. I must have everyone at my little party feel as if they are among family." Ellie had to suppress a chuckle at Lady Dearborn's admonition to her son-in-law, for Lord Glenhaven had indeed executed an exceedingly stiff and formal bow at the introduction. At her words, however, both his body and his expression unbent, and he favoured them all with a very friendly smile.

"Sylvia's word is law here, you know," he said. "Welcome." Lady Glenhaven, a petite young woman with soft brown hair and eyes, shyly echoed her husband's greeting.

They had scarcely seated themselves before more guests arrived, a Mr. and Mrs. Willoughby and their two sons. As they lived nearby and would not be staying overnight at Huntington Park, there was no need for them to repair upstairs before greeting the others. John and Timothy Willoughby were handsome, fashionable young men in their early twenties who appeared delighted to make the acquaintance of Miss Winston-Fitts and Miss O'Day.

As introductions were made all round, Forrest had leisure to observe Rosalind as she interacted with the others. Their week's separation had not dimmed her beauty in the least, he was pleased to note. If anything, being deprived of her company for a time made him appreciate looking at her all the more. He decided not to hurry her into conversation, that the effect might last longer.

Surveying the other guests, his eye was caught by Miss O'Day. She looked devilishly fetching in that summery blue gown, he thought. Really, she was not so plain after all. He was seized with a sudden desire to hear her musical laugh again.

"If I were to arrange a few tables of whist one evening, do you suppose Mrs. Winston-Fitts would allow your uncle to play?" he said quietly, moving to her side.

As he had hoped, she chuckled aloud. "If you were to invite him personally to do so, I doubt she would dare to gainsay you. I dare swear you might even prevail on *her* to play a hand or two, if she thought it would please you."

Lord Dearborn smiled. "I would far rather induce *you* to play, Miss O'Day. I promise to keep the stakes low."

Ellie sketched him a mock curtsy. "Then I shall look forward to it, my lord."

His attention was drawn off then by Mrs. Winston-Fitts, who had a question about the extent of the gardens. It did not suit her in the least that he had spoken to Elinor before paying proper homage to Rosalind.

"I have no doubt my mother will be delighted to take you on a tour of the gardens tomorrow, ma'am," he said in answer to her query, "for they are her especial pride. In fact, I suspect that it was partly in hopes of showing them off that she arranged this little party."

The countess immediately launched into a discussion of the glories to be found in the gardens of Huntington Park, promising to guide anyone interested on a full exploration of them on the morrow. "You *must* see my roses, ma'am," she assured Mrs. Winston-Fitts. "I have been told that they rival those at Malmaison."

A short time later, after the arrival of Lady Emma Childs and her daughter from London, the tea tray was brought in for the refreshment of the assembled company. At the heels of the footman trotted two coal-black cats, their attention riveted on the treats he carried.

"Charm! Token! Come here, my pussums!" cooed Lady Dearborn. "Did you manage to escape from Mrs. Hutchins? So clever, my pets, but naughty, naughty!" Gathering the pair onto her lap, she turned apologetically to her guests. "They really are not allowed in here, but they *will* slip away to find me. I generally take tea in my rooms with all my pussies, and Charm and Token have quite come to depend on me to share little titbits with them."

So saying, she proceeded to break off bits of salmon from a sandwich to feed to her little friends, though she was firm that they eat it on the floor rather than her skirts. Once they had received their due, one cat jumped back to its mistress's lap to curl up for a nap, while the other curiously explored the unfamiliar room and its equally interesting occupants. One or two people offered the cat a crust, but it would not deign to take anything from anyone but the countess. After winding in and out among the chair legs with feline grace, it finally selected a suitable lap: Rosalind's.

"Here, puss, puss! You are Token, are you not?" Ellie moved quickly, intercepting the cat just before it landed on her cousin's lap. The startled animal extended its claws, but retracted them immediately as she began to stroke it behind the ears. A rumbling purr emerged from its throat.

The countess, nothing if not observant, noted Miss Winston-Fitts's white, strained face and asked, "My dear, do you not care for cats?" There was just a hint of alarm in her voice.

Rosalind stammered something inaudible before Mrs. Winston-Fitts broke in. "My daughter has not much experience with them, my lady, that is all," she said hastily. "No doubt she will grow accustomed to them in time." She looked at the cat Ellie held as she spoke, and her lip unconsciously curled in distaste.

"How could you possibly know that was Token, Miss O'Day?" demanded Forrest, seemingly unaware of the sudden strained silence. "I vow, I can never tell them apart."

"His eyes are golden, while Charm's are more green," she replied, grateful to him for deflecting the countess's and her aunt's attention from Rosalind and her discomfort. "I noticed it when your mother introduced them."

"Why, how clever of you, my dear!" exclaimed Lady Dearborn, eager to put the awkward moment behind them. "I daresay you are the only one in the house besides myself to have noticed that!"

The tension effectively broken, the conversation swelled again to the volume it had enjoyed before the entrance of the cats. The countess breathed a sigh of relief. It was obvious that Miss Winston-Fitts was more than a little nervous of her precious pussies, and she didn't care to think what might have happened had Token actually landed in her lap. She was pleased that her guests had not been so discomfited, and knew that she owed the smoothing over to her son and, even more, to the quick-witted Miss O'Day. As Forrest continued his conversation with the little brunette, Lady Dearborn regarded her with sudden interest.

CHAPTER TEN

"FORREST, IS THERE any gentleman friend of yours that you'd care to invite out before my little ball next week?" asked the countess that night as she prepared for bed, having summoned her son to her boudoir. "Lady Emma had hinted that she and Prudence would not be coming, but here they are, after all, and now my numbers are off. We need two more gentlemen. The vicar will do for one, but I can think of no one else in the neighbourhood."

Forrest gently dislodged a calico cat from the purple velvet settee and seated himself, steepling his fingers thoughtfully. "As a matter of fact, Mother, there is. Sir George Bellamy. I met him at Lady Sefton's—decent chap, very likable. A neighbour of the Winston-Fittses, I believe."

Lady Dearborn directed a searching gaze at her son. "An admirer of your Rosalind, perchance, or of Miss O'Day? By the by, I like that girl," she informed him.

"Which one, ma'am?"

"Well, both of them, of course, but I was referring to Miss O'Day. She showed great presence of mind this afternoon, as well as an understanding of cats. I don't know that *I'd* have realized in time what Token meant to do, and certainly I'd not have been quick enough to prevent it. Why did you not warn me that your Miss Winston-Fitts was afraid of cats?''

"I had no notion of it. It was not a subject that naturally arose in our conversations."

"Nor did many others, I'll be bound," surmised the countess. "She hasn't much to say for herself, has she?"

"I believe she shows a very becoming modesty, not putting herself forward as so many young ladies are wont to do." It was Forrest's turn to watch his mother. She was only echoing what his own thoughts had frequently been, especially of late, but he felt obliged to defend Rosalind nonetheless.

"Perhaps you are right. I can scarcely claim to know the girl yet, though certainly she is lovely enough. The two of you should have the most beautiful golden-haired children..." Her words trailed off as she imagined the prospect.

"You go too fast, Mother," Forrest interrupted her happy musings. "I have not yet offered for her, remember."

Lady Dearborn hesitated before replying, picking up a large, fluffy white Persian and stroking it thoughtfully. "Her mother tells me you danced with her three times at Lady Allbeck's last week," she finally said. "You should not have done so, Forrest, if you do not intend to follow through with an offer. Whether Miss Winston-Fitts expects it or not I cannot say, but her mother most assuredly does, and I believe you can count on her to tell the world if you jilt her daughter now."

"Yes, yes, I know all that," said the earl irritably. "However, standing up with her that third time was... Well, at any rate, I *do* intend to offer for her. She is very beautiful, is she not?" His eyes almost pleaded for reassurance.

"Indeed she is, as I have already said. However, there is more than that to a happy marriage, as I am sure you are aware. Your happiness means more to me than golden-haired grandchildren, Forrest. If you do not love her, you should not marry her. It is as simple as that." She forced herself to speak bracingly. She *did* so want those grandchildren!

"And what of your Madame Fortunata?" asked Forrest, not altogether jokingly. "Would she not warn me against flouting my 'Destiny'?"

The countess was nonplussed. She had almost forgotten that she was the one who had instigated this whole business, with her suggestions to Cora for her son's "fortune."

"Destiny has a way of working itself out," she finally said. "The path is laid before your feet, whether you see it or not. You must simply do what you think is best—and right." She prayed that Miss Winston-Fitts, as insipid as she appeared on the surface, might indeed have the capacity to make her son happy. If he married her and was miserable, she would never forgive herself.

"Thank you, Mother. That is precisely what I intend to do," he replied, rising to go.

It was not until he reached the door to his own bedchamber that he remembered Sir George. Why the devil had he asked his mother to invite the man? For

Miss O'Day's sake? After having observed them to-gether during his last two weeks in London, he no longer believed that she had any real partiality for him, nor he for her. Besides, the thought of Ellie O'Day married to Sir George Bellamy did not bring nearly the satisfaction he had thought it would. Ah, well, it was done now. He would wait to see what came of it.

He wondered why had he not told his mother the truth about that dratted third dance at Lady All-beck's. Was he simply too embarrassed to admit that it had been a mistake? When Mrs. Winston-Fitts suggested that he might enjoy a second dance with her daughter, he had absent-mindedly agreed, completely forgetting that he had already danced twice with her—as Mrs. Winston-Fitts had no doubt intended!

His dances with Rosalind must not have been especially memorable, he supposed wryly, if he were able to forget one so easily. Still, he was now in honour bound to offer for her—not that he was disinclined, of course. She would make him an admirable wife. It simply rankled to have the decision taken out of his hands. Sighing with an unnamed discontent, he prepared for bed.

The countess, meanwhile, had also remembered her son's suggested guest. He had never answered her question, she recalled, but now it scarcely seemed to matter. Destiny would do what it would, and perhaps this Sir George would be a tool for it. Hanging a pierced stone on the bedpost as she always did to prevent nightmares, she climbed into bed, willing, for the moment at least, to let Fate take its own course.

"I vow, I could spend all day tending the flowers had I no other responsibilities," said Lady Dearborn to her guests as she guided them through her gardens the next morning. "Have you any hobbies or interests, my dear?" she asked Rosalind. Determined to get to know her, she had kept the tall girl by her side during the tour.

"Er, not . . . not really, ma'am," Rosalind replied nervously, not meeting the countess's eyes.

"Indeed." Disgruntled at yet another setback, for she had been trying for half an hour to draw Miss Winston-Fitts out, Lady Dearborn turned to Miss O'Day, who walked just behind. "How about you, dear? Do you care for gardening at all?"

The question caught Ellie by surprise, but she answered readily enough. "I adore anything that allows me to be out of doors, my lady. Riding, walking, even astronomy, which my father taught me. Gardening, however, is a particular passion of mine. I do so miss my mother's rose gardens." Her smile was sweet, but wistful.

The countess regarded the girl's heart-shaped face and intelligent grey eyes with approval. "You must see mine, then, and tell me how they compare. Perhaps you might have a hint or two for their care that I have not heard." She ushered the group, which consisted of her feminine guests, along with Forrest and the two Willoughby sons, through an opening in the high, thorny hedge that divided up the gardens.

"Oh, Lady Dearborn! How magnificent!" gasped Ellie as they rounded the corner to see the rose gardens spread before them. The other ladies *oohed* and *aahed* appropriately, but the countess privately thought Miss O'Day's response the only sincere one.

"What think you, Miss O'Day?" she asked. "Would your mother have liked my roses?"

"She would have been in heaven," Ellie replied simply. "We did not have anything to compare to this. Why, you must have two or three dozen varieties here, at least!"

"Forty-one, actually," said the countess with pardonable pride. "I began collecting them shortly after my marriage to Forrest's father, thirty-two years ago."

"Yes, I can recall more than one summer trip to the north for that express purpose," remarked the earl. "Not to mention France. Most women go to Paris for the fashions. My mother goes for the rose cuttings!"

This drew a general chuckle, but Ellie said, "And see how much more she has to show for her travels than they do!" She was still looking about her in delight. "I see now where the inspiration for the Rose Room came from."

"Oh, yes, Forrest suggested that room for you, Miss O'Day," said Lady Dearborn, with a quick, piercing look at her son. "He must have known of your fondness for roses."

Ellie glanced at the earl, who was looking self-conscious, and then at her aunt, who was frowning. Rosalind appeared not to be attending to the conversation at all. "I believe I may have mentioned it to him once. How astute of you, my lord, to remember. And how kind." Lord Dearborn met her glance then, and something in his look made her drop her eyes in confusion.

"Well!" said the countess briskly, deliberately breaking the mood. "Shall we proceed to the herb garden?"

The group continued on their tour, John Willoughby managing to secure a place at Miss Winston-Fitts's side while his brother walked along next to Miss O'Day, soon drawing her into an animated discussion of the countryside. Forrest followed along at the rear of the group, trying to decipher his feelings.

What was it about Miss O'Day, he wondered, that made him so enjoy pleasing her? Was it simply that she was so easy to please? She had been sincerely grateful to him for the simple favour of selecting a room that he thought she would like. He could not think of another woman of his acquaintance who would have appreciated, or even noticed, such a small kindness. There was more to it than that, though. There was something about the girl that made him *want* to please her. At first, he had thought it was merely pity, combined with his admiration for her gallant spirit. Now, however, he began to suspect another motive in himself, one he was not certain he wanted to probe too deeply.

For one thing, there was Miss Winston-Fitts to consider. He had noticed, and approved, his mother's attempts to become acquainted with Rosalind, but had noted, too, her singular lack of success. What he had first taken as praiseworthy modesty and reserve in her manner, he had by now come to realize was, in fact, paralysing shyness. He also had begun to suspect—disloyal thought!—that his lovely Rosalind did not possess a first-rate intellect. These were flaws that might become severe disabilities in a future Countess of Dearborn. Forrest thought of all of the duties his mother took upon herself—social, charitable and managerial, both here and in Town—and, try as he might, he could not imagine Rosalind Winston-Fitts one day assuming them.

Shaking himself free of such disturbing thoughts, he saw that the rest of the party had gone on some distance ahead. Hurrying to catch them up, he thrust his introspections aside for the time being.

"...far superior to dried herbs, I assure you," the countess was saying as he rejoined the group. "Did you not notice how savoury the sauce for the sole was last night? Cook says he could never manage it without this garden."

"My daughter has a light hand with herbs, my lady," Mrs. Winston-Fitts put in quickly. She, too, had noticed the countess's efforts to draw Rosalind out, and could have shaken her daughter for her lack of response.

"Does she?" Lady Dearborn turned towards Miss Winston-Fitts with a smile. "That is certainly what is needed."

"Yes," went on Rosalind's mother, "she used to help in our herb garden when she was younger." She forbore to add that she herself had forbidden her to continue once she turned sixteen, deeming it an unladylike pursuit. As the countess obviously did not consider it so, Mrs. Winston-Fitts was only too willing to change her opinion on that head.

"I hope you remember to keep some of your rosemary planted at the doors. 'Tis very lucky to do so.

What other talents is she blessed with?'' asked Lady Dearborn, apparently deciding that the mother was a more likely source of information than the daughter.

"Oh! She does the most exquisite needlework imaginable,'' responded Rosalind's proud parent. "Why, even Elinor here has said that her work is like that of fairies.''

"Very true, my lady,'' concurred Ellie eagerly. "My cousin can make nigh invisible stitches. Her patience and precision amaze me, for I can never sit still long enough to do a piece of work to even my own satisfaction, much less anyone else's.'' Despite her own conflicting feelings regarding the forthcoming match, Ellie very much wanted Rosalind to get on with her future mother-in-law. Unfortunately, however, the countess seemed less than impressed.

"I fear needlework has never been one of my strengths,'' said Lady Dearborn. "I, too, find myself unable to sit at something so mindless for very long.'' Then, seeming to realize what she had implied, she quickly added, "It is a most admirable and feminine accomplishment, however, and one to be commended.''

"Quite so,'' agreed Mrs. Winston-Fitts with a barely perceptible sniff.

"Here we have our little apple orchard,'' said the countess, plainly eager to change the subject. "The blossoms are past their prime now, but they were quite spectacular a fortnight ago, I assure you.'' She was interrupted at that moment by an unearthly wailing from above.

Looking up, Ellie saw an orange tabby cat far out on the limb of a nearby apple tree. He had apparently gone out farther than he had intended and was now fearful of retracing his route, although he was actually no more than six or seven feet from the ground. As she watched, the cat emitted another pitiful howl.

"Oh, gracious!" exclaimed Lady Dearborn. "It would be Red Devil. Forrest, I don't suppose you would..."

"That monster took a swipe at me just last night," protested the earl. "He's a foul-tempered beast. Oh, all right, Mother," he relented at the pleading look she sent him. Reaching up to where the cat clung just over his head, he crooned, "Come, puss, puss. Come on, then."

The cat, unappreciative of Lord Dearborn's charitable intentions, hissed menacingly and let go one forepaw to swat at the outstretched hand, claws extended.

"I've no intention of letting this brute injure me, Mother," the earl informed her, withdrawing his hand. "He may stay there till he starves, with that sort of attitude."

John Willoughby stepped forward. "I'll give it a try, m'lady, if I may," he said confidently. "Watch this, Miss Winston-Fitts," he added to Rosalind with a wink. Easily topping six feet, he was an inch or two taller than the earl and his face was nearly on a level with the cat when he stood on tiptoe. "Now you just come down, Mr. Red Devil," he ordered loudly, reaching up with a quick motion to seize the animal by the scruff of the neck.

Red Devil, however, had other ideas and twisted round like lightning to sink his teeth into Mr. Willoughby's wrist. The young man let go with a howl not unlike those that the cat had been uttering before.

"Bloody ungrateful beast!" he cried. "Hang there, then!" The cat flattened his ears and hissed again.

"Oh, dear," said the countess. "I should have warned you, John, that Red Devil tends to be a bit nervous around strangers."

Forrest guffawed at this understatement. "Nervous? Vicious is more like it, and *I'm* certainly no stranger to him!"

"I suppose we should let him calm down a bit. Perhaps he'll come down on his own if left alone," said the countess worriedly. The group obligingly moved away, but Lady Dearborn glanced backwards several times to where the cat had resumed his cries.

"Might ... might I try, ma'am?" asked Ellie diffidently. She very much feared that she might appear to be showing off, and she knew for certain that her Aunt Mabel would not approve, but the animal's distress bothered her nearly as much as it plainly pained its mistress.

"He really is a most intractable pussy, Miss O'Day," Lady Dearborn cautioned her. "And however would you reach him?" Like the countess herself, Ellie stood barely over five feet tall.

"If one of the gentlemen would be so kind as to pull that chair over, I could stand on that," she replied, nodding towards an ornamental wrought-iron bench that stood against the hedge. Timothy Willoughby moved with alacrity to do her bidding, though Forrest was obliged to help him before the bench was properly positioned beneath the tree.

"I really must advise you against this, Miss O'Day," said the earl earnestly as she prepared to step onto it. "My mother found that cat running wild when he was half-grown, and he's never been quite tame. I would never forgive myself were he to injure you."

"Nor I, my dear," agreed the countess. "I'm not at all certain that naughty kitty deserves such a risk on your part."

"Certainly not!" chimed in Mrs. Winston-Fitts. "I pray you will refrain from making a spectacle of yourself, Elinor, and come away at once!"

"You needn't watch, ma'am," Ellie informed her sweetly. "In fact, I will no doubt go on much better without an audience." Lady Dearborn's concern for the cat was evident, and Ellie had resolved to do what she could. "I promise to be careful, my lady," she assured her hostess, climbing onto the bench.

Mrs. Winston-Fitts, incensed to have her orders flouted by her niece but unable to do anything more while the countess supported this mad scheme, turned to go back to the house. "Very well," she said tightly. "If it is as you say, we had best leave you alone with the beast, I suppose. Come, Rosalind."

Rosalind followed her quite readily, only too willing to leave the cat's vicinity. Accordingly, the two Willoughbys and their mother came along, as did Lady Emma, Prudence and Lady Fenwick. The countess and her son remained behind, however, much to Mrs. Winston-Fitts's vexation.

Ellie waited until the majority of the group had left the orchard to turn her attention to the cat, now less than a foot above her. Making little chirruping noises, she reached up very, very slowly, pausing anytime the cat reacted by so much as twitching an ear. "Go-o-o-od Devil, swe-e-et Devil," she crooned softly, advancing her hand until she could stroke him between the ears. Still he did not flatten them, so she stroked further, smoothing the ruffled fur along his spine. As she felt him relax, she reached up with her other hand until she could cradle him between them. He clung to the branch for a moment, but then apparently decided to trust his weight to her and came away easily enough. Ellie stepped down and handed him to the countess.

Lady Dearborn set him down quickly after a brief hug caused him to struggle. It appeared that even his mistress had little control over Red Devil. "I don't know how to thank you enough, Miss O'Day. He might very well have got down on his own, but I would have fretted about him all day. You have quite a knack with cats, it would seem."

"I used to play with the barn cats all the time when I was a girl, and most of them were at least half-wild," explained Ellie, suddenly shy. "I learned that avoiding any sudden movement was the surest way to win their trust."

"I'll certainly remember that the next time I have dealings with the Devil," said the earl, laughing. "Why did you not warn me of that earlier, Mother?"

"I must confess, I had not thought of it," replied the countess. "We may have to keep you with us, Miss

O'Day,'' she said teasingly. "You are quite too useful to be without.''

"Indeed,'' agreed the earl, smiling down at Ellie, who was suddenly blushing furiously. "I can't imagine what we ever did without her.''

CHAPTER ELEVEN

AUNT MABEL had been right, thought Ellie, alone in her room a short time later. She should never have put herself forward so. Why, any observer could be forgiven for assuming that she was trying to supplant Rosalind in the earl's affections—or at least in his mother's affections—as Aunt Mabel most assuredly must. And was she, she wondered? Could she truly be so despicable as to deliberately try to ruin dear Rosalind's best chance at a happy marriage? She devoutly hoped not.

She had *tried* to make her cousin appear in a more favourable light to Lady Dearborn, and indeed, what she had said about Rosalind's embroidery was perfectly true. Somehow, though, whenever she tried to help, her efforts seemed to backfire and only draw that much more attention on herself. She could not be completely sorry for helping that poor cat, of course, and she knew that the countess had been sincerely grateful, but Lord Dearborn had seemed more amused than anything else. What had he meant by agreeing with his mother that they should "keep her with them?"

Had Rosalind perhaps suggested to him that she stay on as her companion after their marriage? As much as

Ellie loved Huntington Park, the cats and even the countess, she knew she could never bear that. No, when the earl had looked down at her with an almost tender smile in his eyes, she had realized once and for all that she could never regard him merely as a friend. And where did that leave her? Sighing, she seated herself at the pretty pink-and-gold dressing-table to tidy her hair before nuncheon.

It was a pity that none of her especial admirers had been invited to the house party, she supposed, although the idea of marrying any one of them did not much appeal to her, particularly now. Still, what else was there? Timothy Willoughby had shown her some attention, she thought dispiritedly. Perhaps she ought to encourage him. Of course, that would still mean living in the neighbourhood of Huntington Park, if not on the estate itself.

"You're being a very poor sort of cousin," she told her reflection aloud. "You should be focussing your energy on ensuring Rosalind's happiness, not on your own wretched future! There will be time enough for that later." A sudden vision of the empty years stretching ahead almost made her quail, but she straightened her back and raised her chin defiantly. "Perhaps I *could* induce Lord Dearborn to fall in love with me—though I doubt it," she said to the image in the glass. "But I would hate myself forever for it. Whoever else may share my future, I shall always have to live with myself!"

NUNCHEON WAS a lively meal, in spite of Mrs. Winston-Fitts's marked coolness towards her niece. Timothy Willoughby was frankly impressed, and his brother even more so, at the earl's recital of Ellie's rescue of Red Devil.

"Are you certain you are not hiding bites and scratches beneath your gloves, Miss O'Day?" asked John. "If not, you must be quicker than I."

Ellie repeated what she had told the countess, that slow movements rather than quick ones were what made the difference. As she spoke, she glanced at Lady Dearborn, who had been listening to another recital of Rosalind's accomplishments from Mrs. Winston-Fitts. At Ellie's words, however, she turned.

"Yes, Miss O'Day was quite wonderful. We must think of a way to keep her with us, I think," she said, echoing her words in the orchard, as Ellie had half feared she might.

"Oh, you must have her to stay on as Rosalind's companion, then, should a certain happy event take place," suggested Mrs. Winston-Fitts quickly. "My daughter has quite come to depend on her, as well, you must know, for Elinor has often proved herself useful." Her tone put Ellie firmly in her place as a poor dependant.

"An excellent notion!" exclaimed Forrest from across the table. It irritated him to hear Mrs. Winston-Fitts speak so of her niece, and his only thought at the moment was that in his household she need never be subjected to such humiliation again. Not until he saw the odious woman's smirk did he realize that he had essentially admitted in front of them all that he planned to make Rosalind his bride.

Ellie flushed scarlet with mortification. Between them, her aunt and Lord Dearborn were conspiring to force her into precisely the impossible situation she was determined to avoid! In desperation, she said, "I'm certain Rosalind can get along perfectly well without me. Indeed, I hope she can, for I plan to accept my grandfather's offer to live with him in Ireland in the very near future." With great effort, she managed to keep her voice steady.

"Oh! Have you heard from Lord Kerrigan, then, Elinor?" asked her aunt, momentarily diverted from savouring her double triumph. Not only had the earl all but declared himself just now, but he had offered to take her irksome niece off of her hands, too.

"Your grandfather is Lord Kerrigan, Miss O'Day?" interposed the countess before Ellie could answer. "Lord Kerrigan of Kerribrooke? I knew him rather well in my youth. He was quite the charmer, as I recall. How does he go on these days?"

"He . . . he has been ill, my lady, but I believe he is mending now." Ellie prayed that this might be the truth, though she really had no idea, as the offer she had just alluded to was entirely fictitious. "His heir, Lord Clairmont, has been seeing after the estates."

"And Lady Kerrigan?" prompted the countess with a half smile. "He married Miss Alice Winchell, I remember. She and I were bosom rivals in those days." Her eyes took on a faraway look.

"I'm afraid Grandmama went to her reward nearly five years ago, Lady Dearborn," said Ellie quietly, reluctant to cause her hostess pain. She had never been as close to her grandmother as to Lord Kerrigan, but vividly recalled her father's grief at her passing.

"Poor Alice. She always was a sickly thing—the die-away, delicate sort that some gentlemen prefer. As for me, I could dance till dawn and still be up for a gallop before breakfast. Then, of course. I don't say I could do so now." Her tone clearly indicated that she believed she could, however, and Ellie saw no cause to doubt it. Lady Dearborn had shown herself to be possessed of remarkable energy for a woman of her years.

"So Kerrigan is on his own, is he?" the countess continued. "I must send a letter of condolence about Alice, and tell him how much I like his granddaughter." She nodded decisively.

Ellie could not suppress a smile. "Thank you, my lady," she said warmly. "He will appreciate it, I know."

"As I was saying, ma'am," broke in Mrs. Winston-Fitts at this point, apparently deciding that she had been ignored long enough, "Rosalind was the wonder of the county for her singing. Perhaps we might open your instrument tonight after dinner if any of the young ladies—or gentlemen—play."

Lady Dearborn allowed that she was not averse to such a scheme and the conversation turned to more general topics, to Ellie's relief. She silently thanked the countess for her inquisitiveness about Lord Kerrigan, which had prevented her from being forced to reply to her aunt's query about his supposed letter. Perhaps *some* good would come of her little deception, she mused. If Lady Dearborn actually wrote to him, and mentioned her in her letter, the longed-for invitation might finally come. She hoped so, for she would sooner live without a roof over her head than under the same one that sheltered a newly—and undoubtedly happily—married Lord Dearborn and Rosalind.

THAT EVENING, after a dinner of surpassing excellence, the company assembled in the drawing-room. The gentlemen had lingered only briefly over their port, eager, no doubt, to discover what the countess had planned for their evening's entertainment.

"Forrest said something earlier about a few tables of whist," she began, "and as there are sixteen of us, we can just fill four. However, we may do that another evening just as well." Lady Dearborn glanced about, gauging the reactions of her guests to this suggestion. She dearly loved a game of whist herself, and had even been known to prevail on the Hutchinses to make up a table when Forrest was at home.

"Did you not earlier mention the possibility of music, my lady?" Mrs. Winston-Fitts ventured when no one else seemed likely to suggest an alternative to a vulgar evening at cards. "Perhaps one of the young people could be prevailed upon to play for us, and Rosalind, I know, would be delighted to sing." She was determined to display her daughter to advantage, and singing was Rosalind's one real talent, apart from embroidery.

"Oh, very well, I suppose I did," replied the countess, thinly concealing her disappointment. "As I said, we may play at whist just as well tomorrow night. Prudence, would you care to play?"

Lady Emma nudged Miss Childs forward, nearly as eager to show her daughter off before Lord Dearborn as was Mrs. Winston-Fitts. She had been trying to bring Prudence to the earl's notice for years and had nearly given it up, but he was not betrothed yet. And, of course, there were the two young Mr. Willoughbys, both respectable husband material, to consider.

Ellie watched the two young ladies with sympathy, for it was perfectly obvious, to her, at least, that neither had the least desire to perform. Rosalind, she thought, should be used to it by now, for her mother had been putting her forward like this since she had discovered her daughter's singing voice at the age of fifteen. Judging by Miss Childs's resigned expression, she had been similarly prodded by her ambitious mama on frequent occasions.

The performance was pleasing, if not spectacular, and after listening awhile, Ellie was able to conclude that her aunt had better cause for encouraging her daughter's exhibition than did Lady Emma. Rosalind's voice was sweet and true, as always, but poor Prudence's playing was scarcely above average and served mainly as a vehicle for Miss Winston-Fitts's singing. That Miss Childs knew it as well became obvious when, after only two or three songs, she stood and declared herself fatigued.

"Someone else, surely, can play for a bit so that I may more fully enjoy Miss Winston-Fitts's performance," she suggested. It was apparent that she shared none of her mother's aspirations and preferred to end her own part in the proceedings as soon as possible. Ellie warmed to the girl instantly and went to sit beside her.

"You did very well," she said in an undertone as Timothy Willoughby took over at the pianoforte.

"You are most kind, Miss O'Day," replied Prudence, pushing her mousy brown hair away from her rather plain face. "I don't know why Mother always insists that I play, for she cannot reasonably believe others will be impressed by it."

Mr. Willoughby's playing was, if anything, inferior to Miss Childs's, but he continued gamely for a song or two, until Mrs. Winston-Fitts, apparently feeling that her daughter would appear to better advantage with a more skilled accompanist, applied to Lord Dearborn.

"My lord, surely you play?" she asked. "I vow, there is no better way to pass quiet evenings at home than in music, one partner playing and the other singing."

Lord Dearborn was obliged to shatter this picture of domestic bliss by replying, "I fear I never developed my skill beyond the most elementary level, ma'am. My voice is better suited to display than are my fingers, I fear."

"Then you and Rosalind must sing a duet," suggested Rosalind's fond mama instantly. "Elinor, perhaps you would take a turn at the instrument." Her reluctance to allow her niece to put herself forward was overshadowed by her desire to place Rosalind and the earl in such close, and doubtless romantic, proximity.

Ellie reluctantly advanced to the pianoforte. She had no doubt that she would perform creditably, for she had excelled in music before her parents' death, though she had had few occasions to play since. But she hated to cast poor Prudence Childs in the shade, especially so soon after befriending the girl.

At the first strains of a lively country air, it would have been difficult to say who was more surprised. Ellie's playing was little short of brilliant, especially contrasted with the indifferent performances which had preceded hers. And Lord Dearborn revealed himself the possessor of an exceptionally fine baritone singing voice which he used to great advantage in the rollicking tune. Ellie listened to him with delight, scarcely noticing the approving look he cast her way. Rosalind's voice blended sweetly with the earl's, Ellie noticed, but she refused to let jealousy interfere with her delight of the music.

Spurred on by the excellence of the singers, Ellie felt that she had never before played so easily or so well. At the end of the song, the other guests, along with Lady Dearborn, broke into spontaneous applause.

"That was marvellous!" exclaimed the countess. "What a good idea this was, Mrs. Winston-Fitts. Come, let us have another!"

The trio obliged, Ellie varying the tempo from brisk to slow and sweet, and then back again to a country reel that set everyone's toes to tapping. At the end of the third song, Rosalind shyly declared herself to be out of breath, looking to her mother for permission to stop.

"Very well, I suppose that is enough for one evening, sweetheart," answered her proud parent. Her plans were moving along well and she was in charity with the world at the moment. "You might stop as well if you like, Elinor," she said almost kindly to her niece.

"Are you fatigued, Miss O'Day?" asked Lord Dearborn, looking down at her with raised eyebrows. "I confess, I was just beginning to enjoy myself."

"I am perfectly willing to continue if you are, my lord," she said readily. "Rosie began before either of us, so she has some excuse for retiring." Her intention was to turn the earl's attention back to her cousin, for she was finding his steady regard unsettling, but she failed of her object.

"Do you know any Irish airs?" he asked, continuing to gaze at her face. Ellie nodded and launched immediately into one of her favourites so that he would be forced to sing before her colour could rise any further and perhaps excite the suspicions of her aunt.

The two of them continued at the instrument until the tea tray was brought in, in spite of several attempts by Mrs. Winston-Fitts to lure Lord Dearborn back to her daughter's side. Nor could she prevail on Rosalind to sing again, but was forced to watch the very tableau she had envisaged at the pianoforte, only with different characters.

To increase her chagrin, Lady Dearborn commented at one point, "How well they perform together! Why did you not tell us at once how well your niece plays, Mrs. Winston-Fitts?"

She was forced to make a vague disclaimer about letting the other young people participate, realizing

that Elinor was in danger of eclipsing Rosalind yet
again, this time without opening her mouth. The
knowledge that she herself had suggested the evening's entertainment, and Elinor's playing in particular, did nothing to soothe her temper.

"IT WAS QUITE SELFISH of you to monopolize the instrument all evening, Elinor," said Mrs. Winston-Fitts
to her niece as they retired to their rooms for the night
an hour or two later. "I daresay Miss Childs would
have been happy of another chance to perform."

Her hand already on the doorknob to her chamber,
Ellie started and turned at this unexpected attack.
"Lady Emma might have been, but Prudence most
certainly would not," she informed her aunt with
more honesty than wisdom. "She told me herself how
she detests being forced to play before company. At
any rate, it was at your request that I began, and at
Lord Dearborn's and his mother's that I remained.
Would you have had me refuse?"

Ellie was still exhilarated by the experience of accompanying the earl, and even more so by the approving—and at times, something more than approving—looks he had cast her way during their recital. She had not yet had time to analyse her feelings,
but knew that she felt more alive than she had in years.
Thus, she was more than usually willing to defend
herself against her aunt's unjust accusations.

"No, of course you could not refuse," replied Mrs.
Winston-Fitts ill-naturedly. "But you might have
feigned fatigue rather than show off, as dear Rosalind did."

Ellie shot a glance at her cousin, wondering if she would refute her mother's assumption; but Rosalind, though looking somewhat nettled, said nothing.

"Very well, ma'am," Ellie finally said, her high spirits fading. "I will attempt to take your advice in future. Must I also feign ignorance of whist, if we are to play tomorrow night, as Lady Dearborn suggested?" She could not quite keep the note of bitterness from her voice, but her aunt seemed not to notice.

"Whist! That reminds me," said Mrs. Winston-Fitts, diverted. "You must spend tomorrow morning teaching Rosalind to play, for it will never do for Dearborn to discover that she is ignorant of the game. He appears quite fond of it, and she will doubtless be expected to play occasionally after their marriage."

Ellie felt her spirits sink further at this reminder. "Of course, Aunt Mabel. Shall we meet just after breakfast, Rosie?"

Rosalind agreed with a show of enthusiasm that put the finishing touch to her cousin's sudden depression. It was obvious to Ellie that Rosalind wished to please the earl by learning the game, which could only speak of her growing affection for him.

"I'll see you in the morning, then. Good night, Aunt Mabel, Uncle Emmett. Good night, Rosie." With an effort, she kept a smile on her face. Gone was her pleasant plan of reliving her musical evening as she drifted off to sleep, recalling every glance, every word, that the earl had directed her way. She now wanted nothing more than to crawl into bed and sleep, preferably without dreams.

CHAPTER TWELVE

ROSALIND'S INSTRUCTION at whist had to be put off
the next morning when the countess suggested a tour
of some other parts of the estate. Ellie, along with
Rosalind and her parents, had just served themselves
from the ample selection on the sideboard when their
hostess breezed in, turquoise scarves and orange
feathers flying, to acquaint them with her plans.

"The grounds on the western side of the house are
well worth seeing," she informed them, "and there is
a very pretty duck pond that I am persuaded you will
like, Miss Winston-Fitts. I have been meaning to walk
over that way myself, in any event, for I must have a
look at the dower house before ordering its refurbish-
ing." This was said with a suggestive look at Rosalind, which she missed entirely as her eyes were on her
plate. The significance was by no means lost on her
mother, however.

A short time later, everyone but the Fenwicks ventured out: the ladies to see the beauties the grounds
offered and the gentlemen, at Forrest's suggestion, to
discover what the fishing might be like. The countess
set a surprisingly brisk pace, and the group arrived at
the dower house in under ten minutes. Ellie looked
eagerly about her as they went, revelling in the feel of

soft, springy grass beneath her feet and the warm, rich scents of early summer.

"Here we are," said Lady Dearborn cheerily as they came within sight of a handsome half-timbered house. "I vow, I can scarcely wait to live here. I have always wished to be a dowager, you know," she said conspiratorially to Mrs. Winston-Fitts, but in a voice loud enough for all to hear. "Then my eccentricities might be more readily excused. I have enough of them, goodness knows!"

Ellie glanced at the earl as his mother spoke to see how he would react to her blatant prodding and was diverted to see his colour deepen. Never one to dwell on her own disappointments, she could not help smiling at Lady Dearborn's humour and her son's discomfiture at it. Lord Dearborn caught her amused glance and grimaced in response, rolling his eyes at his mother's words. Ellie stifled a giggle and quickly looked away, lest the others—her aunt in particular—notice and question the nature of their private joke.

As the countess moved ahead, she heard Mrs. Winston-Fitts murmur to Rosalind, "There, my dear! Doubtless Lady Dearborn will take all her beastly cats along with her to the dower house once you are married." Ellie suddenly lost any desire to laugh.

After a brief tour of the dower house, which was of handsome proportions, if in need of redecorating, the ladies went on to see the duck pond while the earl led the gentlemen in the direction of a small lake fed by the stream they had crossed on their first approach to the house. As she had the day before, the countess attempted to draw Rosalind out of herself, but with no more success. Meanwhile, Ellie was striking up a friendship with Lord Dearborn's sister, Lady Glenhaven.

"Teddy loves to come here for the fishing," Juliet confided to Miss O'Day after the gentlemen departed. "He would spend the entire summer here in that pursuit if he did not need to attend to his own estates, I believe."

"My father was fond of the sport, also," Ellie told her, "and I must admit that I rather enjoy it myself, though I have not had a chance to fish, of course, since I was quite a child." She was liking Lady Glenhaven very well. Though she was nearly as shy as Rosalind, what little of her conversation she had so far heard showed her to be both intelligent and informed.

"Do you really?" Lady Glenhaven was delighted. "I did so as a girl, as well. Perhaps the two of us might slip out one morning to indulge—I believe my old tackle box and poles are still in the stables."

Ellie had just acceded to the plan when Mrs. Winston-Fitts called out for her to keep up. She wrinkled her nose at her aunt's peremptory tone, which caused Juliet to choke with laughter. With a final smile for her new friend, Ellie trotted to Mrs. Winston-Fitts's side to echo any praises she might utter on her daughter's behalf for the remainder of the tour.

"NO, NO, ROSIE! You have to follow suit!" Though normally patience itself with her cousin's slower understanding, Ellie was growing increasingly exasperated after nearly an hour of trying to explain the rudiments of whist to her. "Really, you must attend."

"Perhaps I won't play tonight, after all," said Rosalind, pushing her cards to the centre of the table with a sigh. "I cannot seem to grasp it at all."

"But I thought you wished to learn, to please the earl and his mother," Ellie reminded her, gathering up the cards so that she could deal them out again. She had intended to go over a hand or two with all cards showing, and then ask her aunt and uncle to make up a table for a few practice games, but Rosalind was not yet ready for that step.

"I thought I did, too, for it sounded like fun. But I had no idea it would be so *difficult*."

"It's not—well, never mind. It is almost time to dress for dinner. Perhaps you can sit out tonight and we can try again tomorrow." Ellie had no real enthusiasm for another attempt just then, either.

THAT EVENING, the countess was determined not to be put off again. Really, it had been ages since she had enjoyed a good game of whist! She had invited the vicar for dinner that evening solely because he was one of the best players she knew of, barring Forrest and herself, of course. Therefore, when the ladies entered the drawing-room after dinner, four tables had already been set up at Lady Dearborn's express orders.

"How went Rosalind's lesson this afternoon, Elinor?" asked Mrs. Winston-Fitts in an undertone, seeing the inevitable before her.

"Not well, I'm afraid, Aunt Mabel," Ellie confessed. "I fear she is by no means ready to play against anyone of skill." *Or anyone who understands the rules,* she added silently.

"How can that be? The two of you were closeted together for an hour!" her aunt hissed. "You said you knew the game. I am most disappointed in you, Elinor." Lady Dearborn directed a comment her way just then, and Mrs. Winston-Fitts turned with a brittle smile. "I beg your pardon, my lady. Of course, we shall all be delighted to play."

"Excellent!" The countess beamed. "Lady Emma is feeling poorly, and wishes to retire early, but with Mr. Marsh here, we will have just sixteen." In truth, from something Forrest had told her, she had expected Miss Winston-Fitts, and possibly her parents, to beg off, as well. The news that Forrest's Rosalind could in fact play came as a welcome surprise to her.

The gentlemen came in a few minutes later, and Lady Dearborn immediately appropriated Mr. Marsh, the vicar, as her partner. "Forrest, perhaps you and Miss Winston-Fitts would like to play at our table," she suggested. That would allow her to gauge the level of her future daughter-in-law's play.

To her surprise, however, Forrest responded, "I'll be happy to be your opponent, Mother, but it will have to be with Miss O'Day as my partner. I have already promised to test her skill at the game. Perhaps we can mix up the tables later on," he added as an afterthought, suddenly realizing that his response might appear to slight the girl he had all but offered for.

As they took their places, he whispered to Ellie, "I thought you said Miss Winston-Fitts and her mother did not play," with a significant nod to the table where all three Winston-Fittses were seated with John Willoughby. The elder Willoughbys were seated opposite Sir William and Lady Fenwick, while Miss Childs and Timothy Willoughby challenged Lord and Lady Glenhaven.

"I can't answer for Aunt Mabel, but I cannot but sympathize with Mr. Willoughby as Rosalind's partner," Ellie whispered back, "for I gave her her first lesson in the game this afternoon. Perhaps in actual play she will pick it up fairly quickly." This last was said more in the spirit of complimenting Rosalind to her future husband than from any conviction that her words might prove true.

The countess called their attention to the game at that point, and Ellie was soon completely absorbed in the play. The years since she had last played seemed to melt away as she kept careful count of the cards as they were laid on the table, theorizing which ones were likely left in which player's hand. The mathematics at which she had always excelled as a girl stood her in good stead in the game, just as it had contributed to her skill at the pianoforte. When points were counted up at the end of the hand, Ellie and Lord Dearborn were well in the lead.

"It is a good thing the stakes tonight are imaginary, or we should owe my son and Miss O'Day a small fortune, Mr. Marsh," said Lady Dearborn when the earl and Ellie made game a few hands later. "Forrest, why did you not warn me that we had an expert in our midst? I vow, I don't believe you misplayed one card, Miss O'Day."

"I was dealt good hands, my lady," Ellie disclaimed. "I do enjoy whist, though. It was my father's favourite game."

"And his father's, too, as I recall," replied the countess with a reminiscent smile. "Lord Kerrigan was a formidable player when he was young, and I do not doubt that he has improved with age."

Soon after that, the assembled party stopped to take some refreshment before sitting down again with different partners. This time, Ellie was partnered by Juliet, playing opposite the Willoughby brothers, while Lord Dearborn reluctantly teamed with Miss Winston-Fitts to play opposite her father and the countess. Mrs. Winston-Fitts was successful in persuading the Fenwicks and Prudence Childs to sit out and observe for a while.

"Perhaps I can win back some of what I have lost," said John Willoughby cheerfully as he seated himself. "To think I grumbled about the stakes being imaginary tonight!" He shook his head and groaned.

"You'll not win any back if we can help it, John," said Lady Glenhaven with the easy banter of long familiarity. "The ladies will win the day, you'll see."

Unfortunately for the Willoughbys, she was correct. Juliet was no mean player herself and her skill, combined with Ellie's, allowed the brothers very few points, though the dealing, if anything, was in the young men's favour.

"We make a good team, do we not?" she asked as she tallied up their winnings after a final, hard-fought hand. "You had best take care, Miss O'Day, or Mama will never let you leave Huntington Park. She is constantly alert for good whist players to add to her circle.''

Ellie returned a suitably light remark, but she could feel her insides contracting. More and more, it looked as though she was to be forced to stay here after Rosalind's marriage, and much as she was growing to love the house and its inhabitants, she could think of no fate more certain to bring her constant pain. She prayed that the longed-for invitation from her grandfather might come soon.

"ARE YOU CERTAIN you have no clubs?" Forrest asked Rosalind as she played a six of hearts on the five of clubs he had led.

"Oh, yes, I suppose I do." She picked up the card she had played and replaced it with the king of clubs, which he had been fairly certain she held. As a matter of fact, she had misplayed so many times, that he had seen nearly every card in her hand by now—as had their opponents.

"Our game!" said the countess triumphantly at the end of the hand. "We must be about even now, Forrest. Let me see . . . yes, I have won back all but a hundred pounds." As always when the stakes were fictitious, they were playing for exorbitant sums. "Another game?"

"I'm willing," said Mr. Winston-Fitts at once. He was enjoying himself enormously, in spite of his daughter's abysmal performance.

"Would you care for a walk in the gardens, Miss Winston-Fitts?" asked the earl, desperate to do anything rather than continue with her as his whist partner. "Perhaps the Fenwicks would care to play some more."

The transition was quickly arranged, and Rosalind picked up her shawl, obviously as eager as Lord Dearborn to leave the card table. Forrest led her to the end of the room and opened one of the long French doors leading onto the terrace.

"I see we have nearly a full moon tonight," he remarked conversationally. "Mother will want everyone to stay until after the new moon, I imagine, so that they can travel more safely."

"Is...is it dangerous to travel after the full moon?" Rosalind was startled into asking.

"Just unlucky," replied Forrest with a smile. Really, she did look lovely in the moonlight—almost lovely enough to make him forget his irritation over her card-playing. "My mother is a consummate expert on all things pertaining to luck, as you will no doubt discover."

"Oh," said Rosalind softly, turning slightly away from him to gaze across the moonlit gardens.

Suddenly, Forrest realized that he had unwittingly created the ideal opportunity to propose to her. The moon, the gardens, everything was romantic perfection. He cleared his throat, but then stopped. Unaccountably, Ellie O'Day's face arose before his mind's eye, and he suddenly knew that he was not ready to commit himself to the beautiful but slow-witted girl beside him.

He thought of Ellie spending the afternoon trying to teach Miss Winston-Fitts to play whist, and his heart went out to her. He was certain he could never display so much patience himself—and, as Rosalind's husband, surely that and much more would be required of him. He would have to make her understand the running of his estates, her social obligations, even the balancing of a table of dinner guests. He was not at all certain that he could face the prospect. He imagined a lifetime of explaining the simplest matters, over and over, to his wife and felt suddenly tired.

"It is rather cool. Would you like to go back inside?" he asked abruptly. He knew full well that his mother, the Winston-Fittses—in short everyone—was expecting him to offer for Rosalind, but he couldn't do it. He was not certain how he might honourably withdraw his suit, but do so he must. He knew now that he could not sacrifice his life's happiness for the sake of propriety, honour—or even his supposed "Destiny". With a suddenly light heart and a spring in his step, he led Miss Winston-Fitts back into the house.

ELLIE MISPLAYED her first card of the evening. Her entire attention was on the probable scene outdoors, where Lord Dearborn and Rosalind had disappeared a moment ago. She knew that her aunt had been contriving to get the two of them alone almost from the hour of their arrival at Huntington Park, but it appeared that this romantic tête-à-tête had been the earl's idea, and not Aunt Mabel's. Ellie had no doubt that an announcement of his and Rosalind's betrothal would be made shortly, perhaps that very evening.

"Ellie, dear, spades were trumps on the last hand," Juliet chided her gently. "This time around it is diamonds." The sympathetic look in her eyes told Ellie that Lady Glenhaven had somehow divined her secret.

Hastily pinning a carefree smile on her face, Ellie apologized for her absent-mindedness and picked up the errant card. She forced herself to focus on the game and was enjoying some measure of success in spite of her thoughts when she saw Rosalind and Lord Dearborn re-enter the room, less than five minutes after they had gone out. Searching their expressions, she saw little to indicate that anything momentous had just occurred. Lord Dearborn, perhaps, looked happier than he had on their exit, but Rosalind looked as vague as ever—certainly not like a girl who had just received a proposal of marriage.

Breathing somewhat more easily, Ellie was once again able to attend to the game and she and Juliet quickly regained the points they had lost owing to her earlier lapse. She was just thinking what a pity it was that the fifty thousand pounds she had won tonight were not real when the sound of the front door knocker interrupted everyone's play.

"Gracious! Whoever could that be at this hour?" wondered Lady Dearborn aloud.

A moment later, her question was answered by Hutchins, who entered to announce in stentorian tones, "Sir George Bellamy."

Ellie had never been more astonished, but the countess was already rising to greet her new guest, and Lord Dearborn stepped forward with perfect cordiality. Neither of them seemed in the least surprised at their visitor's identity—only at the lateness of his arrival.

"I had begun to fear you could not come, Sir George," the earl was saying jovially. "Mother would have been most upset, for she particularly desired to make your acquaintance."

Ellie glanced towards Rosalind to gauge her reaction to her erstwhile suitor's entrance and was pleased to see that she appeared composed, if rather pale. After completing his greetings to his host and hostess, Sir George came forward to make his bows to the Winston-Fittses, then seated himself next to Rosalind, whose colour changed from white to bright pink and then back as Ellie watched.

Peeping involuntarily at Lord Dearborn, where he still stood next to his mother, Ellie was mystified to see a small, satisfied smile playing about his mouth.

CHAPTER THIRTEEN

ELLIE HAD little opportunity to unravel the state of even her own feelings, much less those of the earl or Rosalind, during the next few days. Lady Dearborn's ball was quickly approaching and she had offered her help in the preparations, help the countess had been eager to accept. Her advice was sought on such small matters as the types of flowers best suited to the various rooms and the rearrangement of the furniture in the great hall to effect its transformation into a ballroom. Likewise, she helped to write and address the invitations that were to be issued to all the neighbouring gentry. She would have enjoyed her various tasks more if the thought had not kept recurring that the ball's main purpose was to introduce the next Countess of Dearborn—Rosalind—to the surrounding county.

Rosalind, meanwhile, took no part in the numerous preparations for an event that might be thought to have some importance for her. Mrs. Winston-Fitts, no doubt seeking to conceal her daughter's shortcomings at penmanship, went so far as to praise Elinor's hand to the countess in recommending her for the post of writing out invitations. And, of course, when an opinion was sought as to the decorations, Rosalind could never be prevailed upon to offer one. Ellie often feared that she appeared too outspoken by contrast, but Lady Dearborn never failed to praise her taste when she made her preferences known.

In fact, a warm affection was growing between Ellie and Lady Dearborn, so much so that Ellie was distressed at the thought of leaving Huntington Park, though she could not regret her decision to do so. She saw little of the earl during this time, for the weather was fine and the gentlemen were abroad most days, but her thoughts were never far from him. After most of a London Season, Ellie had had ample opportunity to compare Lord Dearborn to a great many other high-ranking and handsome gentlemen and could unequivocally say that he was far superior, both in person and address, to all of them. Of course, she could no longer claim to be completely impartial in her judgement, for she had finally admitted to herself that she had fallen in love with him.

She had not tried to do so. In fact, she had very definitely tried *not* to, but it seemed that she had no more control over her emotions where Lord Dearborn was concerned than she had over the direction of the wind. By keeping her hands and thoughts occupied in assisting the countess with her preparations, she hoped to at least distract herself from the unenviable state in which she found herself, of loving a man destined to another.

Thus, it was with mixed feelings that she responded to Juliet's suggestion, two days before the ball, that they slip away after an early breakfast for a few hours of fishing. Ellie knew that Lady Glenhaven at least suspected her feelings for her brother and feared that she might try to force some sort of confession from her during the course of the morning. At the same time, it would be a vast relief to confide her inner conflicts to another.

"I have already had Jim, the stable-boy, bring my old tackle round to the kitchen," Juliet said, her soft brown eyes sparkling with mischief and excitement. "Mama will not need you till after nuncheon, for she is to meet with Forrest and the steward this morning. 'Twill be the perfect opportunity."

Her enthusiasm was contagious, and Ellie promised to meet her at the kitchen door in fifteen minutes. Running upstairs, she changed into an older gown and sturdy walking shoes, snatched up a light wrap and hurried back down, her heart surprisingly light at the thought of a brief escape from the problems that kept hammering at her. She would not think about the earl at all while they fished, she promised herself.

Ellie discovered quickly that her promise had been rash, for the two young ladies were not even out of sight of the house before Juliet said, "Forrest seems very preoccupied these days. Have you any idea what might be troubling him?" Her tone was casual and her eyes were on the path ahead, but Ellie suspected that she was sincerely concerned about her brother.

"I—I have seen very little of Lord Dearborn of late," she replied in as calm a voice as she could manage. She thought back over the past few evenings, when she had used the task of addressing invitations as an excuse to avoid watching him and Rosalind together after dinner. "Perhaps he is anxious that the ball come off well," she suggested.

"Oh, pooh!" Juliet dismissed that idea. "Forrest never concerns himself with that sort of thing. He knows perfectly well that Mama will pull off another social triumph, as always. Speaking of the ball, however, why is it that your cousin is not more involved? From what Mama says, it will likely be her engagement party, as well. I should think she'd be thrilled at landing a catch like Forrest, but she seems quite detached about it all. Perhaps she is merely shy, however." She watched Ellie closely as she spoke.

"Rosalind is certainly shy," Ellie was able to agree with complete honesty. She endeavored to hide her pain at Juliet's words, but the earnest gaze her friend directed at her told her that she had not been completely successful.

Juliet did not immediately comment on her observations, however, but drew Ellie's attention to a bend in the stream, where it widened into a pool beneath some overhanging willows before continuing on its way. "This used to be my secret fishing spot when I was a girl," she said. "I actually only remember catching one fish here, but it was my favourite place whenever I wished to be alone. Here, let us spread this out on the ground here, and bait our hooks." She shook out an old bedspread she had brought along for the purpose while Ellie dealt with the fishing gear.

When they had settled down side by side, their lines in the water, Juliet said quietly, "You've grown rather fond of Forrest, have you not?"

Ellie flushed, but nodded. "I find Lord Dearborn very...agreeable," she said with an effort. "I'm certain he will make my cousin very happy." She stared blindly at the water, refusing to meet Juliet's eyes.

"Oh, Ellie!" Juliet burst out unexpectedly. "I don't *want* Miss Winston-Fitts as my sister! I would much rather have you."

Ellie turned in surprise at her outburst to find Juliet's eyes as damp as her own. "Please, Juliet, you mustn't—" she began, but Lady Glenhaven cut her off.

"I had promised myself to say nothing of this, but I can't help it, Ellie," she said plaintively. "I cannot seem to get two words out of Rosalind, and I have tried. I know what it is to be shy, for I have always been so, and I don't hold that against her. But I could swear she does not love my brother." She chewed her lip for a moment before adding, "Oh, how can Forrest be so blind? Surely he must see that someone like Miss Winston-Fitts can never make him happy. Why, she has no sense of humour at all that I can perceive, and Forrest loves a good joke above anything! If he could only see past her pretty face, he might find that the perfect match for him is right before his nose."

Ellie felt it absolutely necessary to stop her now. "Juliet, I pray you, say no more," she pleaded. "My only consolation has been that they might be tolerably happy together. Do not take away the one thing that might save me from complete misery."

"Then you *do* love him!" exclaimed Juliet triumphantly. "I was almost certain you did. And your cousin does not." She stated it as fact.

"I—I don't know that to be true," said Ellie hesitantly.

"Well, I do, for I have been watching her closely. She seems far happier in Sir George Bellamy's company than in Forrest's. And what is more, I don't believe Forrest is in love with her, either. Oh, he admires her, of course, but that is not at all the same thing. Hmm—let me see..." Her words trailed off as she lost herself in thought.

"Juliet, you must say nothing of this to anyone, especially your brother!" cried Ellie in alarm. "Promise me! Even if they are not exactly in love yet, that does not mean they may not grow to love each other in time. And I assure you, my aunt is quite determined to see this match, and no other, take place. She will make poor Rosie's life quite wretched if she does not marry Lord Dearborn." The very thought of the earl learning of her own feelings put her in a quake. So far, she was certain that the object of her love was completely unaware of it—as he must remain.

"As if your cousin will lack offers," said Juliet pettishly. Then, catching Ellie's pleading glance, she relented. "Oh, very well, I will say nothing. Perhaps Forrest will come to his senses on his own." The smile that accompanied her words did not reassure Ellie at all, but she had no choice but to accept Juliet's promise at face value.

The two ladies turned their talk to other matters for the remainder of their fishing expedition and both found it a pleasant exercise even though they caught nothing. Ellie noticed Juliet's speculative gaze upon her once or twice during lulls in the conversation but refused to agitate herself by attempting to guess her friend's thoughts.

She could not afford to allow Juliet's words to give her false hope—even if Juliet was correct about Lord Dearborn's feelings towards Rosalind, that did not mean that he was any more likely to fall in love with *her,* she thought unhappily.

As THE PREPARATIONS for the ball were nearly complete, Ellie had no excuse to avoid the after-dinner gathering in the parlour that evening. It was with some trepidation that she awaited the entrance of the gentlemen, for this would be her first opportunity, not counting mealtimes, to see Lord Dearborn and Rosalind together since her talk with Juliet that morning. She was not certain whether she hoped or feared to confirm Lady Glenhaven's opinions with her own observations; she only knew that discovering the truth was of vital importance to her.

Lord Dearborn's first words on his entrance were not designed to add to her peace of mind.

"Let us have some music tonight, shall we?" he said to the company as soon as they were all assembled. "Miss O'Day, will you oblige us at the instrument while your fair cousin favours us with her voice?"

Ellie and Rosalind acquiesced readily enough, the former catching her aunt's look to remind her not to remain at the pianoforte for too long. The two of them performed creditably, and Ellie, stealing surreptitous glances in his direction, saw that the earl's gaze was fixed on them the entire time; but whether he was looking more at Rosalind or herself she could not have said for certain.

At Mrs. Winston-Fitts's urging, Lord Dearborn came forward after the second song to sing a duet with Rosalind. Feeling herself suddenly unequal to watching them perform together, Ellie stood up. In as playful a tone as she could manage, she said, "Sir George, perhaps you would care to play for a while. I recall that you are by no means unskilled."

She received a small, guilty satisfaction in knowing that she was obeying her aunt's strictures while at the same time creating a situation that Mrs. Winston-Fitts was unlikely to relish.

Sir George looked uncomfortable at being singled out, but stepped forward without undue hesitation to take her place. The earl joined Rosalind at the pianoforte, and Sir George struck up a lively melody. Ellie thought that Rosalind sang more sweetly than before, but did not know whether to credit the improvement to Sir George's presence or Lord Dearborn's.

"Sir George has not quite your skill at the pianoforte, but he seems to bring out the best in our singer, don't you think?" asked Lady Glenhaven at Ellie's ear, startling her.

She turned quickly. "They often performed together in Warwickshire," she replied, willing her colour to remain normal. "No doubt that is an advantage."

Juliet allowed that it might be so, and they listened in silence for a moment. Suddenly, Ellie felt that she could bear no more.

"I—I am feeling a trifle warm, Juliet," she whispered apologetically to her companion. "I believe I shall step outside for a breath of air. I shan't be long." Willing herself to walk slowly when she felt far more like fleeing the scene, Ellie made her way to the French doors at the rear of the room.

The guests were standing and sitting in groups, some engaged in low conversation, as Sir George and the two singers began another song. Mrs. Winston-Fitts frowned as her niece moved past her, and Ellie responded with a carefree smile that quite belied her nervousness.

Glancing back as she silently opened the door, Ellie was thankful to see that her aunt's attention had already returned to the trio at the pianoforte. She slipped outside and breathed a sigh of relief before gulping deep draughts of the cool night air. Forcefully, she banished the picture of the two golden heads blending their voices so beautifully inside. She would think only of the darkened scene before her.

"THAT WAS LOVELY, Forrest, Miss Winston-Fitts," said Lady Glenhaven at the conclusion of the song. "And you play quite excellently, Sir George. In fact, you have induced me to try my voice tonight. Might I join you, Miss Winston-Fitts? I'm certain Forrest won't mind sitting one out." She had noticed his eyes following Ellie's exit from the room and hoped that he would take advantage of the opportunity she was giving him. Juliet had never enjoyed singing before company, but she felt that the present circumstance justified the sacrifice.

The earl took her cue with commendable smoothness. "Not at all, Juliet," he said. "It has been an age since I've heard you sing," he continued, with a significant glance that she hoped no one else noticed, "and I'm certain you and Miss Winston-Fitts will sound like two songbirds together." He moved away from the instrument with an alacrity that Juliet thoroughly approved. Even more promising, less than halfway into their song she saw him moving surreptitiously towards the doors.

Forrest was indeed grateful for his sister's interference. He had been hoping for two days now to find an opportunity to speak to Miss O'Day privately—to thank her for her efforts on his mother's behalf, of course. Watching Miss O'Day as she left the room, he had thought she looked troubled. Surely it behooved him, as host, to discover what was bothering one of his guests? So telling himself, he made his way, with occasional pauses to speak to one or another of the company, to the doors through which Ellie had so recently disappeared.

Glancing about, much as Ellie had, to be certain that everyone—and Mrs. Winston-Fitts in particular—was attending to the music, he opened one of the doors and stepped out onto the terrace. He did not see Ellie at first, for she had moved some way down the terrace and stood absolutely still, leaning against the railing and gazing steadfastly up at the sky. Forrest watched her earnest profile for a moment before advancing.

"Miss O'Day?" he said softly. "Are... are you feeling quite well?" She started and turned when he spoke, but looked away too quickly for him to be certain whether the sparkle in her eyes was due to tears or merely the moonlight.

"Yes, my lord, I am perfectly all right. I merely felt a bit warm, but I thank you for asking." Forrest thought he heard the slightest quaver in her voice, as though she fought to control it. Something welled up in his heart that was not precisely pity or concern, though it had elements of both.

"I have been wishing to tell you how much I appreciate the effort you have undertaken to ensure the success of my mother's ball. No doubt she has thanked you already, but I wished to add my gratitude to hers." His speech sounded rehearsed to his own ears, and he groped for words that might better express his sincerity.

"Your mother has been most kind to me, my lord, and I am happy that I have been able to repay her generosity in some small way." She did not sound happy, though, Forrest thought. He suspected again that she had been crying before his appearance.

"I saw you were studying the skies when I came out. Do I recall you once mentioning an interest in astronomy, Miss O'Day?" he asked, hoping to divert her thoughts from whatever was distressing her.

"Yes, my father taught me," she replied, speaking more steadily now. "I was trying to trace out some of his favourite constellations, but the moon is too bright tonight for good observations."

Forrest glanced up. "Yes, it is exactly full, is it not? I am surprised my mother has none of her superstitious rituals planned for the occasion." He was suddenly struck with the parallel between the present scene and the one he had shared with Miss Winston-Fitts only three nights earlier. There was one major difference, however—on this occasion he felt no inclination whatsoever to hurry inside.

Ellie was smiling now. "Yes, Lady Dearborn has shared some of her, ah, beliefs with me. I will own she is superstitious, but she does no one any harm by it. You speak as though she practices witchcraft." In truth, she had found the countess's various tokens and rites both amusing and endearing.

"Certainly not that," replied the earl with a chuckle. "Indeed, most of her charms seem designed to avert it. But if you had grown up forbidden to eat blackberries after Michaelmas or to stir out of the house on Childermas Day you'd not be so quick to call her superstitions harmless!"

Ellie had to laugh with him at that, and soon he was telling her all about his childhood, and she was sharing much of hers. Their stories were remarkably similar, even though he had grown up surrounded by luxury and she in relative poverty. Both had enjoyed the freedom of outdoor country life and had resented the restrictions adulthood placed on that freedom.

"That is why I so wish my grandfather would invite me to Ireland," Ellie admitted with a sigh, quite forgetting her previous deception to her aunt on that point. "There, I would not be trammelled in by Aunt Mabel's endless rules for proper behaviour."

Forrest moved a step closer to her. "Could you not be happy here?" he asked. "My mother would like you to stay, above all things. She has said so repeatedly."

In spite of the sudden stab of pain at his words, which seemed to speak of his impending marriage to Rosalind, Ellie forced herself to ask the question that had been plaguing her. Raising her chin bravely, she looked him full in the eyes. "And what of you, my lord? Do you wish me to stay?"

Forrest looked down at her upturned face, and everything suddenly fell into place for him. By way of an answer, he took her in his arms and lowered his lips to hers.

Ellie stiffened briefly in surprise, but the temptation to give in, to have this one perfect moment to remember, was too strong. She allowed her lips to soften under his, to revel in the wild sweetness of her very first kiss. Groaning, he pulled her closer and Ellie responded eagerly, putting her arms around his broad back to press herself even more tightly against him. The stars, the moon, seemed to swirl around her as she closed her eyes and gave herself completely to his embrace. She had never imagined such ecstasy.

Forrest gradually felt his reason return and reluctantly released her. He was astounded at his own reaction to that incredible kiss. Why had it taken him so long to realize what this girl meant to him? It all seemed so obvious now, so perfect. Of course, she was what he had wanted all along. How could he not have known it before? How stupid he had been, to think that Rosalind, rather than Ellie, was his "type"! Ellie O'Day was precisely the kind of woman who could make him happy. He opened his mouth to tell her so, but suddenly remembered Miss Winston-Fitts and the expectations he had so foolishly raised in that quarter. In honour, he could not offer for Ellie until that matter was resolved.

"Miss O'Day—Ellie—I—" he began, but she stopped him.

"Please, my lord, you needn't." She backed away from him, both hands pressed to her flaming cheeks. "We must both endeavour to forget that this ever happened. I—I promise not to speak of it to a soul, and I shall leave for Ireland as soon as may be, whether my grandfather writes to me or not. I pray you, do not tell Rosalind what I have done!"

She whirled and ran into the house by another door, while Forrest gazed after her with a bemused smile. He had no intention of forgetting that kiss, or her response to it, nearly as eager as his own. No, he finally knew his heart and he praised Heaven that his eyes had been opened in time, before he had irrevocably committed himself to Miss Winston-Fitts. It was crystal clear to him now that his true Destiny lay with Miss Ellie O'Day and no other. First, he must free himself of that other entanglement and then he would somehow convince her of that.

CHAPTER FOURTEEN

ELLIE MANAGED to reach her room without being seen. Her heart was in her throat as she hurried down the corridors and up the long stairway, for fear that she would be required to explain her flight to someone. Finally closing the door of her chamber behind her, she leaned against it with a sigh of relief, allowing the soothing rose tones of the room to calm her racing pulse. Now that the immediate fear of discovery was past, however, other, even more insurmountable, problems arose to torment her.

How, *how* could she have allowed Lord Dearborn to kiss her and, worse, how could she have allowed herself to respond as she had? She had betrayed Rosalind, who trusted her, as well as her aunt and uncle, Lady Dearborn and even the earl himself. For surely he must right now be feeling a remorse nearly equal to her own. What if her rash surrender to temptation had blasted his chance at a happy marriage with Rosalind? She would never forgive herself!

That thought led to another: why *had* he kissed her? Surely, whispered a small, wicked voice at the back of her mind, it must be evidence that he did not love Rosalind, after all. But no, she would not build up foolish hopes. Most likely, his kiss had merely been meant to reassure her that she would be welcome to stay at Huntington Park after his marriage to Rosalind. A kiss of comfort and pity. It was doubtless her own shameless response that had turned it into something quite different—for there had been a passion, a fire in him that went far beyond pity, and that she could not, even now, dismiss as mere wishful thinking on her part.

But what did it matter? she thought despairingly. What if he did, briefly, feel a spark of desire for her? He was still all but promised to Rosalind, and she had no doubt that Aunt Mabel would make his life and everyone else's miserable if he did not follow through with an offer in form. No, her best course was to do what she had promised, and forget that incredible, terrible, wonderful kiss had ever happened, at least outwardly. She would be as cool and aloof as ever Rosalind had been when next she saw him. But not tonight. No, tonight she would go early to bed and dream, one last time, of the feel of his arms about her, his lips on hers, before banishing such thoughts from her mind forever in the morning.

"AND WHERE WERE YOU, Elinor, when the tea tray was brought in last night?" asked Mrs. Winston-Fitts waspishly across the breakfast table the next day. "Surely you did not remain out of doors until bedtime?"

"No, Aunt Mabel," replied Ellie with tolerable composure, rearranging the food on her plate to make it appear as though she had eaten more than the few bites she had felt able to manage. "I had the headache. I thought that the fresh air would revive me, but when it did not I went up to bed early.'' She had had ample time, since awakening well before dawn, to concoct a reasonable excuse for her disappearance.

"Hmph," her aunt snorted. "Well, it was very rude of you not to take leave of Lady Dearborn before absenting yourself. I thought I had instructed you better than that."

"I shall apologize to her later this morning," Ellie promised, cutting her ham into minuscule pieces before placing one carefully in her mouth. "I'm certain she will understand." Lady Dearborn would never understand if she knew the true reason, Ellie thought. She knew that the countess was looking forward to her son's betrothal to Rosalind nearly as eagerly as Aunt Mabel was. Guilt assailed her anew and she nearly choked on the ham.

"I suppose you do look rather pale," Mrs. Winston-Fitts grudgingly admitted when Ellie's coughing fit subsided. "I hope you do not intend being ill for the ball tomorrow night. Keep your distance from Rosalind today, pray, for I will not have her risk contagion."

"Yes, ma'am."

"Ah, here she is now," said Rosalind's fond mama as her daughter entered the dining-room. "If you are finished, you may go about your business, Elinor," she said pointedly to her niece.

Ellie rose and departed quickly after a brief greeting—from a distance—to her cousin. In truth, she was grateful to her aunt for this excuse to avoid Rosalind, for she feared that she might be tempted to pour out the truth if the two of them were alone for any length of time. Ellie thought that Rosalind looked happier than usual this morning, and she had no wish to be the one to change that.

LADY DEARBORN was quite understanding when Ellie came to her a short time later to explain her absence after dinner the night before. In fact, she understood more than she allowed, for she was no blinder than Juliet and had suspected for some days the true state of Miss O'Day's feelings. She had also noticed her son's departure last night—though, thankfully, Mrs. Winston-Fitts apparently had not—and wondered if there might be a connection.

To Ellie, however, she merely said, "Yes, crowded rooms often affect me so, also. I find it most soothing, when I am not feeling quite the thing, to work in my rose garden. Perhaps you would care to do some pruning for me today? If you'd like to cut a basket or two of blooms for tomorrow night while you are at it, I should be most grateful."

As the countess had suspected she would be, Ellie was thankful for an excuse to spend most of the day alone with her thoughts and agreed readily.

Half an hour later, Forrest requested an interview with his mother, which surprised her not at all. In fact, she had lingered in her rooms longer than usual in hopes of it, brushing out the fur of two of her long-haired cats even though they were not really in need of it yet.

"Mother, I—I hope what I have to say will not upset you too badly" was the earl's disquieting introduction. "But even if it does, I cannot retract it. I have decided that I cannot marry Miss Winston-Fitts." He regarded the countess expectantly, obviously braced for a storm of protest.

Instead, Lady Dearborn smiled. "Pray have a seat, Forrest," she said mildly. "I believe we have a few things to discuss."

He perched on the edge of the settee, regarding her warily. "I warn you, ma'am, I have thought this through and will not be dissuaded."

"I can see that," agreed the countess, enjoying the startled look on her son's face. "I only wonder that it took you so long."

Forrest's expression became one of pure astonishment. "But...but I thought you...that—"

"You thought that I was so desperate for grandchildren that I would hurry you into marriage with the first girl you showed an interest in," his mother finished for him. "I will admit, the idea was tempting, especially given Miss Winston-Fitts's beauty." She allowed herself a sigh of regret for the lovely golden-headed grandchildren they would have given her. "But you must know, Forrest, that your happiness comes first with me—though I am not certain that having Miss Winston-Fitts constantly about would contribute much to *my* felicity, either. Your decision presents us with a problem, however."

Forrest nodded. "Her parents. They quite obviously expect me to offer for her."

"Precisely. I would not put it past that odious woman to spread it abroad throughout London that you had jilted her daughter if you do not, and we really cannot have that. Nor would that circumstance appeal to Miss O'Day, I suspect.''

The earl's head came up sharply at that. "Miss O'Day? What has she to do with this?''

The countess merely chuckled. "Very well, you may keep your own counsel there, if you wish. I'll say no more on it.''

Forrest favoured her with a reluctant smile. "You always were too sharp by half, Mother. But for honour's sake, this first matter must be settled before I can do anything about the other.''

"Agreed. I have noticed that Sir George Bellamy appears to have a marked partiality for Miss Winston-Fitts. Perhaps we may make use of that.''

"I had already formed a plan of sorts along those lines,'' replied Forrest, his smile broadening. "Now that I know you will not oppose it, I believe I shall proceed.''

The countess arched a brow, but did not question him further. "Very well, Forrest, I leave you to do whatever you can,'' she said, rummaging in her pockets as he rose to go. "Good luck!'' she called out as he reached the door, tossing him a hare's foot. The earl caught it and turned it over in his hand consideringly, before tucking it into his own pocket.

"Can't hurt,'' his mother heard him murmur as he left the room.

SIR GEORGE had been surprised when his host singled him out to play a game of billiards, but he had agreed readily enough. He had been quite good in his youth, and there was enough competitive spirit in him still to make him desirous of besting the earl in this, at least. It was ironic that he found Lord Dearborn so likable, he mused as he lengthened his lead in the game. Had Rosalind not stood between them, they might have become friends. He never for a moment suspected that the earl was deliberately allowing him points, so small and skilful were the mistakes Lord Dearborn made.

"Your angle is off a bit," offered Sir George helpfully as Forrest barely missed another shot.

"Thank you," replied the earl with seeming sincerity. "I'll work on improving it." After a brief silence while Sir George made his next shot, Forrest said hesitantly, "Perhaps you could offer me a bit of advice on another matter, as well. Actually, it would be advice that I might pass on to a friend of mine with a dilemma."

"Happy to be of any service, of course," said Sir George, preening slightly at the implication that Lord Dearborn valued his opinion. "What sort of dilemma is he faced with?"

"It involves a young lady he greatly admires," replied Forrest, picking up a cloth to polish his stick. "He believes her to return his sentiments, but her family wishes her to wed elsewhere. Someone of greater wealth or importance than my friend, I imagine."

Sir George attempted to conceal his sudden interest by turning to gaze out of the window at the excellent view it offered of the herb garden and maze below. "A fairly common problem, I apprehend," he said nonchalantly. "I once knew a fellow in similar circumstances myself."

"Ah, indeed! And what did that fellow do? Perhaps his example might be of some use to my friend."

Sir George pondered, trying to look as though he were remembering rather than inventing. "Why, he . . . he offered for her, but her parents would have none of him," he finally said rather hopelessly, putting forth the most likely scenario in his own case—assuming, of course, that he ever actually screwed up his courage to make the offer.

"And then what?" prompted the earl. "Did he call the other fellow out? Place his heart at his beloved's feet? Elope?"

Sir George felt a surge of alarm at the first suggestion, but the last two made him more thoughtful. "As . . . as I recall, he told her of his feelings and persuaded her to an elopement," he replied after a lengthy pause. "He held no animosity towards the other fellow, after all."

"A clever solution, I must say." Forrest nodded as though impressed. "And far less bloodthirsty—or illegal—than a duel. I must recommend that course to my friend. He will need to act quickly, for there is reason to believe that the other fellow might offer at any time." Another noticeable flash of alarm crossed Sir George's face. "I have no doubt he will be most grateful for this advice, as I am for your assistance, Sir George."

Sir George was already lost in thought. "Er, happy to be of service, my lord, as I said," he replied absently. His eyes were on the garden again, where he saw Rosalind herself, accompanied by the earl's sister, just entering the maze. He did not notice Lord Dearborn's smile of satisfaction.

"WOULD YOU like me to show you the secret of the maze, Miss Winston-Fitts?" Lady Glenhaven asked as she and Rosalind stepped out into the bright sunshine. Juliet had proposed a walk in the gardens that the two of them might become better acquainted. "It is not especially large, but it is rather intricate nonetheless."

Rosalind acceded to the plan and followed Juliet into the cool, roofless green tunnels of the shrubbery maze.

"Remember to always turn left as you go in," said Juliet, doing so. "Then, take your next two rights." With the ease of practice since earliest childhood, Lady Glenhaven quickly led Rosalind to the centre of the maze, where a charming Grecian folly had been constructed in the grassy square.

"Oh, how lovely!" Rosalind exclaimed without any prompting.

Juliet smiled, sternly resisting a sudden urge to leave the other girl stranded there until she promised not to marry her brother. "It is, isn't it? My grandfather designed it, and the maze, as well. Why do we not sit here in the shade and talk?"

Rosalind regarded her doubtfully, but followed her obediently enough to a stone bench inside the miniature temple.

"Are you enjoying your stay at Huntington Park?" Juliet began, thrusting down her own habitual shyness.

"Yes, very much, thank you," replied Rosalind, not helping her along at all. Juliet had not expected that she would, however, and plunged on gamely.

"I think this house party was a wonderful idea of Mama's. So often, this time of year can be rather dull. I do so enjoy meeting new people." This was not quite true, but she reminded herself of Ellie to reassure herself that she was not telling a falsehood. "You, your cousin, your parents, and of course that charming Sir George Bellamy," she continued, watching Rosalind closely. As she had hoped, she detected a spark of interest at the latter gentleman's name. "You have known him some time, I apprehend?"

"Oh, yes, since childhood," responded Rosalind with more animation than Juliet had yet seen in her. "He frequently dines with my family in Warwickshire."

"How nice. He seems to admire you greatly." This was said with just a hint of a question.

Rosalind coloured noticeably at this. "I—I suppose so... at least, he used to, anyway. At one time, I thought... But it is of no consequence now, I suppose" was her disjointed reply.

"Oh, I would not dismiss such a worthy suitor as Sir George as being of no consequence," said Juliet in apparent surprise. The conversation was going much as she had hoped, thus far.

"Oh, no!" exclaimed Rosalind quickly in dismay. "I did not at all mean that *he* was of no consequence.

I simply meant that now, with, well, you know . . . his admiration of me is not likely to lead anywhere.''

Juliet regarded her companion's downcast face with approval before asking gently, "Do you mean because my brother seems likely to make you an offer?'' Rosalind nodded unhappily. "But you would not be forced to accept him, would you?''

Rosalind looked up at her, eyes bright with unshed tears. "My mother is quite counting on my becoming a countess, Lady Glenhaven. She will never allow me to wed Sir George, even were he to ask, for he has no title. I am very fond of him, but it is all quite hopeless, I fear.''

"Hmm.'' Juliet considered for a moment. "If you and Sir George were to marry without her consent, I daresay she could be brought round in time. What are your father's feelings on the subject?''

"Oh, he likes Sir George well enough, but he will not go against my mother's wishes, I am sure.''

Juliet nodded decisively. She thought she knew now how things stood. "Miss Winston-Fitts, listen to me.'' Rosalind blinked at her firm tone. "It would be folly for you to go down without a fight. You must at least make an attempt to secure your own happiness.''

"What . . . what do you suggest?'' Juliet was pleased to see a glimmer of hope in Rosalind's face. Perhaps the girl had enough spirit to see it through, after all.

"You must speak with Sir George. Induce him to declare himself. Once he has done so, you can surely find a way around your mother's disapproval. Would it not be worth it?''

"Oh, yes!" Rosalind's eyes shone briefly, before clouding again. "But...suppose he does not really wish to marry *me?*" she asked in a small voice.

"There is only one way to find out," said Juliet bracingly. "Your life's happiness is at stake."

"You are right, Lady Glenhaven," said Rosalind, squaring her shoulders resolutely. "I must try."

CHAPTER FIFTEEN

WHEN ELLIE RETURNED to the house from the rose gardens late that afternoon, laden with dozens of the best blooms, her mind was made up. In spite of her determination the night before, she doubted her ability to keep her feelings for Lord Dearborn hidden. Juliet had already guessed them, and now, with the constant memory of that kiss last night to further unsettle her, it was only a matter of time before Lady Dearborn, Rosalind and, worst of all, Aunt Mabel divined her secret. The only solution, therefore, was for her to leave immediately.

She could not journey all the way to Ireland on her own, of course—for one thing, she lacked the funds—but she could at least go back to Warwickshire, to the Winston-Fittses' house. It was only a two hour drive over good roads, she knew, for she had heard Aunt Mabel discussing the convenience of future visits to her daughter, after Rosalind's marriage to the earl.

The only problem that remained to be settled was how she was to get there. She could think of no way of doing so secretly short of stealing a horse, which of course she could not do. At the same time, she had no desire to generally advertise her departure, which would almost certainly require painful explanations to her aunt and uncle, to the countess and possibly even to Lord Dearborn himself. Her best solution, she thought, would be to confide in Juliet, and to ask for her help.

Accordingly, as soon as she had put the flowers she carried into water, Ellie went in search of her friend. Glancing into most of the downstairs rooms with no success, Ellie finally asked Hutchins where Lady Glenhaven might be found and was directed to Lady Dearborn's chambers. There, she found Juliet ensconced on a sofa surrounded by several cats, enjoying a comfortable cose with her mother.

"So, you see," Juliet was saying, "I did what I could to move things in the proper direction." At Ellie's tap on the open door, she broke off and glanced up almost guiltily, Ellie thought.

"Ex-excuse me, Lady Dearborn, Lady Glenhaven," stammered Ellie, suddenly feeling the awkwardness of her situation. "I wished to tell you that I have brought in the roses you asked for, and...I wondered if I might talk to Lady Glenhaven when it is convenient."

"Come in, Ellie, do!" exclaimed Juliet at once.

At the same time, the countess sprang to her feet, saying, "You girls go right ahead and have your talk. I'd like to go down and have a peep at those roses. They are in the basins in the kitchen, I presume?" At Ellie's nod, she swept out of the room, two of the cats dancing in pursuit of her trailing scarves.

"I have been *dying* to talk to you all day!" cried Juliet as soon as her mother was gone. "Whatever

happened last night?'' Her mild brown eyes sparkled
with curiosity.

"Last ... last night?'' Ellie could feel her cheeks
reddening and knew that Juliet noticed.

"After dinner, silly! You may thank me for Forrest's following you outside so quickly, for I made
quite a point of relieving him at the pianoforte so that
he could.''

"Do you mean that everyone knew we were out
there together?'' Ellie's blush deepened to a morti-
fied crimson.

"No, no! Of course not,'' Juliet quickly reassured
her. "I don't believe anyone but Forrest and myself
noticed *you* leaving, and he was quite sly about his
own exit, I thought. But I can see by your face that
something happened. You...you needn't tell me about
it if you'd rather not, though.''

Ellie could see the effort this last sentence cost her
friend and almost laughed. It would be such a relief to
pour her troubles into Juliet's sympathetic ear!
Quickly and quietly, she related her talk with the earl
and the fact that he had kissed her, though she did not
elaborate on her own—or his—response to that kiss.

"I realized at once how foolish I had been to allow
it, and promised him that I would leave as soon as
possible. That is why I need your help, Juliet,'' she
concluded.

"Leave!'' cried Juliet. "Forrest wants you to leave?
I can scarcely credit that!''

Ellie shifted uncomfortably in her chair. "He ... he
never actually said so. It was my idea, and I fear I did
not stay long enough to hear his reply. But you must

see that it is the only way!'' Her eyes pleaded for Juliet's understanding, but her friend was looking obstinate.

''I don't see any such thing,'' she said stubbornly. ''It sounds to me as though you have made a most promising beginning. Surely, it would be sheerest folly for you to go away just as he is coming to his senses!''

''But what about Rosalind?'' asked Ellie. ''Aunt Mabel is quite counting on tomorrow night's ball doubling as her engagement party, and will doubtless make her—and everyone else—miserable if it is not. I could never forgive myself if I were the cause of ruining her chances of a happy marriage with your brother!''

Juliet thought for a moment. She recalled Sir George's sudden appearance in the gardens that morning, as she and Rosalind were leaving the maze. He and Miss Winston-Fitts had remained together after she went inside, both apparently eager to talk together. Juliet had no doubt that if that little romance were to develop, Mrs. Winston-Fitts would be quick to put the blame on Ellie, somehow. Perhaps it would be best if she were out of that dreadful woman's reach until Forrest was well and truly off her hook. Once Rosalind and Sir George reached an understanding— which Juliet refused to doubt that they would—Ellie could have no qualms about returning. She looked up.

''Where did you wish to go?'' she asked.

''SHE'S DONE WHAT?'' Forrest exclaimed after nuncheon the next day, considerably startling Charm and Token, who were curled up on either side of him on the sofa. "Mother, how could you allow her to leave, without so much as a maid to accompany her? Did that odious aunt of hers send her away?"

He had suspected yesterday that Ellie was deliberately avoiding him, especially when she failed to appear at the dinner table, taking a tray in her room instead. When her "headache" persisted through nuncheon today, however, he decided to seek an explanation from his mother, fearing that Ellie might really be ill. The countess, however, informed him with maddening complacency that Miss O'Day had left more than an hour ago for Warwickshire!

"No, I flatter myself that Mrs. Winston-Fitts is even yet ignorant of her niece's departure," the countess answered her son. "That is what Ellie wished, or so Juliet told me. It was actually she who made the arrangements."

Juliet was little more forthcoming when Forrest questioned her a short time later. Ellie had wished to go home, she said, and preferred that no one know of it until she was gone.

"No one?" asked Forrest in mingled irritation and disappointment. "She apparently felt herself able to confide in you, at least. Can you not tell me what was troubling her?" He had hoped that he and Ellie had reached a new level of understanding the night before last, but that seemed not to be the case.

Juliet's voice was sympathetic. "She needed to borrow a carriage, or I don't believe she'd have told even me, Forrest. I had Mills drive her, so you needn't worry for her safety, at least."

Forrest restrained an urge to shake his sister. "But *why* did she go, Juliet? Was it...was it because of anything I did?"

Lady Glenhaven regarded him innocently. "Why, Forrest? Did you do something to her?"

"Confound it, Juliet!" the earl exploded. "What the devil did Ellie tell you?"

"Surely you do not expect me to betray a confidence?" Juliet asked, her brown eyes still wide and guileless. Then, seeing the dangerous glint in Forrest's eyes, she relented. "Oh, very well. After... whatever occurred between you and she two nights past, Ellie feared that her presence here might jeopardize Miss Winston-Fitts's chances of snagging you, my so-eligible brother. She was understandably nervous about her aunt's reaction to any upsetting of her ambitious plans, and wished to be out of her way. And yours, as well, I believe." Juliet thought the tightening of her brother's lips at this explanation boded well for her hopes.

"Hang Mrs. Winston-Fitts's ambitions!" he exclaimed, much to his sister's delight. "I'd not offer for her empty-headed daughter even if Ellie were on the other side of the globe! I must go after her at once."

"You will do no such thing," said Lady Dearborn, entering Juliet's chamber at that moment. "Have you forgotten that you are to host a ball this evening?"

"Blast! The ball! You can get on without me, can you not, Mother?"

"I fear not, Forrest," the countess replied, not without sympathy. "Miss O'Day will be quite safe at her uncle's home for a day or two. Surely you will not leave me to face Mrs. Winston-Fitts alone when she discovers that her niece is gone?'' Her look reminded him that he also had other obligations to resolve.

Forrest chafed at the delay, but realized that his mother was right. To all appearances, he was still Miss Winston-Fitts's suitor. He wondered irritably whether Sir George had lost his nerve since their promising conversation yesterday.

"She's likely to be more upset when she finds I have no intention of marrying her daughter,'' he finally said with a snort. "What with one and the other, we are like to have our hands full with her, I'll not deny. Very well, Mother. I'll stay for the ball, but I promise nothing beyond that!''

He stalked out of the room, leaving his mother and sister to exchange satisfied glances.

As THE CARRIAGE approached the Winston-Fittses' neighbourhood, Ellie fought to control her tears. It would never do to appear at the door with her eyes red from weeping—Mrs. Flynn, the housekeeper, would be alarmed at once and ask dozens of questions.

Dabbing ineffectually at her eyes with the corner of her shawl, Ellie wondered, for the hundredth time since leaving Huntington Park, if she were doing the right thing. Yesterday, she had been so certain that this was her only course. She remembered her conversation with Rosalind last night, which had only served to strengthen her resolve to run away.

Shortly after dinner, Rosalind had come to her room to see if she were feeling better. To Ellie's surprise, her cousin had been flushed and rosy, her eyes sparkling brilliantly, with a happy smile playing about her mouth. Her own mouth suddenly went dry.

"You are in high spirits, Rosie," she said with false cheerfulness. She could think of only one thing that could account for her cousin's sudden happiness. Lord Dearborn must finally have made his offer! Ellie's heart had contracted within her at the thought.

"Yes, I suppose I am," Rosalind fairly chirped. "In fact, I believe I must be the happiest woman alive!"

Ellie felt that she had suddenly turned to ice. "Why... why is that, Rosie?" she had forced herself to ask, only because it would seem odd if she did not.

"Oh, Ellie! I—but no, I mustn't tell you yet. I promised faithfully to say nothing to anyone, even you, before tomorrow night. Please, though, tell me you wish me happy!" Rosalind's eyes had danced with some delicious secret.

All light had gone out of Ellie's eyes, but she managed to convey the appropriate wishes for Rosalind's future. Looking at her radiant cousin, she felt as plain as pudding by comparison. What foolish hopes she had nurtured!

That was when she had resolved once and for all to leave. If she stayed to attend the ball, she would somehow have to pretend pleasure at her cousin's betrothal announcement, no doubt intended as the *pièce de résistance* of the evening. She would never manage it.

Now, though, miles away from the scene of her heartbreak, Ellie questioned her motives. When she left two hours ago, she had felt quite selfless, as though she were martyring herself for the sake of her cousin's happiness. But now she suspected that she was merely being cowardly—and perhaps foolish, too.

Rosalind, she was sure, could never love Forrest as she did, nor did she think he truly loved Rosalind, either. If that were the case, what chance for happiness did they really have? By leaving, rather than staying to fight for his love, was she condemning them both, as well as herself, to a lifetime of misery?

Just a few hours before, she had managed to convince herself that marriage to the earl was still what she wanted for Rosalind, but suddenly she knew it wasn't so. She wanted Lord Dearborn—Forrest—for herself! It was shameful, she knew, but there it was. Only now, when he was lost to her forever, could she finally admit the truth to herself.

For a moment, Ellie considered asking the coachman to turn around but after a brief internal struggle sat back with a sigh. No, what would happen would happen. If that kiss had meant so little to Forrest that he had gone ahead with his offer to Rosalind, then the best thing she could do would be to forget him. And if she were wrong, if he had *not* offered for her cousin, if he had begun to care for her instead, then maybe— just maybe—he would come after her, as Juliet had seemed so confident he would. Setting her chin firmly, Ellie took a deep breath as the Winston-Fitts house came into view.

Standing on the doorstep of her uncle's house a short time later, Ellie watched the Glenhaven carriage out of sight on its way back to Huntington Park and wished again that she were still inside it. But of course that was why she had told Mills to return with the carriage at once—to put just such temptation out of her reach. She had made her decision and must abide by it. Tossing her dark curls defiantly, she plied the knocker.

She had to rap twice more before Mrs. Flynn finally opened the door to stare at her in astonishment. "Why, Miss Ellie!" she cried. "However do you come to be here?" The housekeeper squinted near-sightedly past Ellie into the yard. "Where are the others?"

"I—I am here alone, Mrs. Flynn," Ellie answered. "My aunt and uncle, and Rosalind, are still visiting at Huntington Park, in Oxfordshire."

Mrs. Flynn clucked her tongue disapprovingly. "The missus sent you home, did she, miss? What sort of scrape have you got into this time?"

Ellie had spent some time during her journey trying to concoct an explanation for her return, but the housekeeper's instant assumption that she was here in disgrace seemed more plausible than any idea she had come up with. "Speaking my mind before thinking, as usual," she replied, trying to look properly ashamed. "I never seem to learn."

The woman peered beyond her again. "But how did you get here?" she asked, on finally determining that there was no vehicle to be seen.

"Oh, I sent the carriage back at once, as my aunt requested," said Ellie glibly, glad that she had not allowed Mills to wait, as he had wanted to. "They will need it for their own trip home, after all."

Mrs. Flynn let out her breath gustily. "Well, come on in, then, and I'll have Mary prepare some dinner for you. You must be fair famished. Oh, I almost forgot! A letter came for you just this morning. I thought to send it on tomorrow, but as you're here..." She handed Ellie an envelope from the hall table before picking up her valise and heading for the stairs at the back of the house. "Come on then, Miss Ellie," she said over her shoulder. "We might as well get you settled in before dinner."

Glancing about her old room while she and the housekeeper stowed her few belongings in wardrobe and dresser, she had the eerie feeling that she had never left at all, that the events of the past two months had been but a dream. London, Huntington Park, Juliet, the countess, even Lord Dearborn himself seemed to fade in the face of the stark reality of her familiar tiny chamber with its worn and threadbare furnishings. But even if the room remained the same, she knew that *she* had changed enough to prevent her ever being content here again.

Ellie waited until Mrs. Flynn had gone back downstairs before breaking the seal on her letter. The seal was Lord Kerrigan's and she was relieved, on unfolding the cover sheet, to discover that the letter was indeed from her grandfather and not, as she had dreaded, from her uncle, Lord Clairmont. Also enclosed was another piece of paper, which proved to be a draft for fifty pounds. Reading quickly, Ellie learned that Lord Kerrigan was fully recovered from the malady which had limited his activities for more than two years and that he had only recently learned of her parents' death and her own distressed circumstances. It appeared that Lord Clairmont had kept it from him out of concern for his health, and he devoted several sentences to his irritation at such coddling. The letter concluded with an invitation for Ellie to join him at Kerribrooke, the enclosed draft to cover her travelling expenses.

Ellie slowly lowered the letter. As quickly, as simply as that, her problems were solved! She could leave for Ireland as early as tomorrow if she chose. There, the rolling emerald hills and deep sapphire loughs would surely mend her broken heart in time. Doubtless Lady Dearborn would consider this letter an omen, a sign that there was nothing more to hope for here in England. She pulled from her pocket the iron ring, made from a horseshoe nail, that the countess had given her for luck before she left Huntington Park that morning, and burst into tears.

CHAPTER SIXTEEN

THE PRE-BALL DINNER was a lively affair, owing primarily to Lady Dearborn's vivid recounting of the latest Town gossip, which she had received in a letter that morning from Lady Jersey. When that subject was exhausted, she launched into a humourous recital of her cats' antics and soon had most of the table chuckling. The only glum faces belonged to Mrs. Winston-Fitts and the earl, but it was doubtful that anyone else noticed.

Mrs. Winston-Fitts was feeling very ill used. It was bad enough that the evening of the ball—the ball that was to have been Rosalind's engagement party—had arrived with no hint of an offer from Lord Dearborn. But then she had discovered, only an hour ago, that Elinor had gone back to Warwickshire that morning with never a word to her. She wondered what her niece could be thinking of to leave at such a time, just when Rosalind was likely to have need of her. That she was truly ill, she refused to believe. Such effrontery, too, to borrow Lady Glenhaven's carriage for the journey! If Elinor were here, she would have given her a fine dressing-down on the subjects of etiquette and gratitude.

In her mother's opinion, Rosalind was looking far happier than the circumstances warranted. While she would have liked to believe that her daughter's high spirits were the result of an understanding with Lord Dearborn, one look at the earl's glowering countenance informed her how unlikely that was. Her one comfort was that with Elinor gone, the friendship she had begun to suspect was developing between her niece and Lord Dearborn would be nipped in the bud, to Rosalind's advantage.

An hour later the ball guests began to arrive, having driven from all corners of the surrounding county and even, in a few cases, from London. As they arrived, each sumptuously clad visitor exclaimed over the changes in the great hall, which had transformed it into a ballroom to rival the finest in Town. Even Mrs. Winston-Fitts forced herself to compliment the countess on its appearance.

"Why, thank you, ma'am," said Lady Dearborn. "Much of the credit must go to Miss O'Day, however, for she has been of great help in the preparations. What a pity that she cannot be here tonight!"

Mrs. Winston-Fitts sourly agreed before wandering off to pour her troubles into her husband's less than sympathetic ear. What was to have been the triumphant climax to the Season was quickly becoming the most unpleasant evening she could remember.

Forrest waited until she had departed before joining his mother near the foot of the stairs. "That woman has a face that would curdle milk," he commented, glancing after her. "Whatever did you say to worsen her mood?"

"I merely mentioned how helpful her niece had been with the decorations," said the countess limpidly, drawing a chuckle from her son. "That's better. Your own face stood in need of some sweetening, too," Lady Dearborn pointed out. Just then, the orchestra struck up the first dance.

"Perhaps it would mollify Mrs. Winston-Fitts if you led her daughter out for the first set," she suggested.

"You wouldn't wish me to raise her hopes again, would you?" Forrest teased. "At any rate, I saw Miss Winston-Fitts going upstairs a few moments ago."

"Perhaps she tore a flounce. You can dance with her later, I suppose. I perceive Miss Childs is without a partner, however."

With a grimace, the earl went to do his duty as host.

The evening passed slowly for Forrest. At his mother's behest he danced every set, but each partner's insipid smiles and boring chatter only served to remind him that she was not Ellie. Again, he wondered how he could have been so wilfully blind for so long. No other woman had ever held his interest as she could. Her spirit, her wit, her dauntless courage more than made up for what little she lacked in the way of beauty. What good was a mass of golden hair, after all? It was merely something to fade with age. What Ellie possessed never would. He looked forward eagerly to the moment when he could go freely to Ellie to declare his feelings and ask for her hand.

He wondered again what Sir George was waiting for. He had no doubt that Rosalind would accept the man if he would only offer—any fool could see that she preferred him. With an effort, Forrest suppressed his irritation at the delay. Right now he had to play his part and make certain that no young lady lacked a partner for the next set. Resignedly, he scanned the room, only to see Mrs. Winston-Fitts hurrying towards him.

"My lord!" she cried breathlessly before he could say a word. "Have you seen Rosalind? I cannot find her anywhere!"

Lord Dearborn regarded Mrs. Winston-Fitts with a slight frown, wondering if this might be yet another ruse to get him alone with her daughter. "I cannot recall that I have, ma'am," he answered politely. "No doubt Miss Winston-Fitts is in the supper room or some such place."

"No, my lord, that she is not, for I have looked," replied Mrs. Winston-Fitts indignantly. "I should think you might show more concern for a girl to whom you have paid such marked attentions!"

Forrest sighed. "I have the same concern for your daughter that I would have for any guest residing under my roof, ma'am. No more, no less." He hoped to dash the impertinent woman's pretensions once and for all.

Mrs. Winston-Fitts's chin quivered, but she did not dispute with him. "As host, then, if for no other reason, I pray you will help me to find her. I am most worried."

Examining her more closely, Forrest had to admit she looked it. Thinking back, he realized that he had not danced with Miss Winston-Fitts at all that evening, had not seen her, in fact, since she went upstairs just after dinner. "Very well, then," he said resignedly. "I shall ask my mother if she has any idea where she might be. Perhaps you should see if your daughter is in her room. She may have taken ill."

"Without telling me?" Mrs. Winston-Fitts was obviously affronted at the thought. "My niece may be capable of that sort of thoughtlessness, my lord, but not my daughter. And if she *is* ill, you may be sure she contracted it from Elinor," she added as an afterthought. She started for the stairs.

Forrest sought out his mother and, with some little difficulty, succeeded in extricating her from a lively conversation with Lady Fenwick about remedies for rheumatism, which included such unlikely practices as carrying a potato in one's pocket. Once he had her attention and a modicum of privacy, he acquainted her with Mrs. Winston-Fitts's concern for her daughter.

"No, I can't recall that I've seen her since the ball began, either, Forrest," replied the countess to his question. "Of course, I've been sitting off in this corner for this half hour and more. Your supposition is likely right, that she is gone to her room for some reason or other."

A sudden possibility occurred to Forrest just then, as he recalled Rosalind's high complexion at dinner as well as Sir George's complacent air. He said nothing, however, merely taking the precaution of manoeuvring his mother to the foot of the stairs. He was glad he had done so a moment later when Mrs. Winston-Fitts reappeared above them, ashen-faced and clutching a crumpled sheet of paper.

As she seemed momentarily bereft of speech, Forrest steered her out onto the terrace. Lady Dearborn, following in some concern, asked, "My dear lady, what is it? What has happened?"

"I—I cannot believe it," Mrs. Winston-Fitts stammered at length. Then, more strongly, "I'll not believe it! My Rosalind has more regard for my wishes than that!" Her glance strayed to the paper she held and her shoulders sagged.

"Please, Mrs. Winston-Fitts, you must tell us what is wrong!" prodded the countess when no other information seemed forthcoming.

"Oh, Lady Dearborn!" exclaimed Mrs. Winston-Fitts, turning towards her. "It is worse, far worse than I had thought. She has been abducted, forced to an elopement by... by Sir George Bellamy! My husband—where is he? He must go after them at once!" cried Mrs. Winston-Fitts, wringing her hands. "Surely it is not too late to stop them."

Forrest made a manful effort to control his twitching lips. So, Sir George had taken his own advice, after all! He put his head in through the door and beckoned to a passing waiter, bidding him to fetch Mr. Winston-Fitts at once. "How long have they been gone?" he then asked the distraught woman in front of him, feeling it necessary to make at least a pretence of concern.

"I don't know. Hours, perhaps! I don't recall seeing either of them since the beginning of the ball. I have been in conversation with Lady Emma this hour and more, and only thought to look for her before the supper dance, to see who...that is, whether...but that is neither here nor there! When I went upstairs to check her room, I found this note tucked into the mirror frame!" She held up the paper, but when Lord Dearborn would have taken it from her, she pulled it hastily away, handing it instead to her husband, who joined them at that moment, appearing somewhat the worse for drink.

"She says that Sir George has persuaded her to marry him and that they decided to be off at once. He must have forced her to this course somehow! They must be stopped!"

Mr. Winston-Fitts, perusing the note, raised his eyebrows at his wife's interpretation of its contents but said only "They seem likely to be very happy together, my dear. I see no occasion for rushing off on a wild-goose chase."

"Emmett, stop and reflect, if you are able!" cried Mrs. Winston-Fitts, rounding on him angrily. "To reach Scotland, they must spend at least two nights on the road. Unmarried! My poor Rosalind's reputation will be quite ruined!"

Mr. Winston-Fitts sobered abruptly at this reminder. "I suppose you are right, my dear," he said with a sigh after a moment's thought. "I shall have to go after them. If my carriage can be made ready—"

"No, I'll go," interrupted Lord Dearborn decisively, earning startled glances from the Winston-Fittses as well as his mother. "No offence, sir, but I suspect my chances of overtaking them are rather better than yours."

"Why, how kind of you, my lord!" exclaimed Mrs. Winston-Fitts, her tragic countenance instantly transformed to one of delight. Plainly, she considered the earl's offer fresh proof that he still meant to marry

Rosalind. "I'm sure you can travel ever so much faster than Emmett." Her husband was looking frankly relieved.

"Forrest, are you quite certain...?" Lady Dearborn began, glancing uncomfortably at the beaming Mrs. Winston-Fitts.

"It occurred from this house, Mother. Therefore, I might be said to have some responsibility in the matter." Just how much, he hoped none of them would ever know! "Besides, if I cannot catch them, I daresay no one can." His look lent a certain significance to his last few words.

Lady Dearborn's face cleared as if by magic as she grasped his meaning. Turning to the Winston-Fittses, she said, "We'd best let Forrest be on his way. If we are to hush this up, we'll need to put our heads together to come up with a plausible excuse for your daughter's absence." With a ghost of a wink at her son she hustled them away.

FORREST WHIPPED UP the team of the landau carriage with profound relief. Miss Winston-Fitts's elopement had given him a perfect excuse to go after Ellie far earlier than he had hoped. So eager was he to reach her side that he would have ridden rather than driven, had not his ostensible errand prevented it; Mrs. Winston-Fitts would doubtless have protested his returning her daughter on horseback.

Of course, Forrest had not the slightest intention of continuing north past Birmingham to Gretna Green. Miss Winston-Fitts might marry whomever she wished, with his heartiest blessings. The thought made him pause. Examining his feelings, he could detect no inkling of regret for the woman who had held him spellbound for the past two months. No, Ellie had completely cured him of that silly, and nearly disastrous, infatuation. All he wanted to do now was to lay his heart before his beloved's feet and apologize for his previous stupidity.

This journey, therefore, served a twofold purpose. Not only would it bring him to his sweet Ellie before morning, but it should put off any other pursuit of Miss Winston-Fitts and Sir George, allowing them to complete their elopement in peace. Since he himself had suggested it, Forrest thought that it was the least he could do. He still marvelled, however, that the strait-laced Sir George had actually brought himself to do something so unconventional as eloping. It seemed so completely out of character.

Such thoughts as these served to while away his journey. He felt not the smallest twinge of guilt as he passed the turning for the road north and continued on towards Birmingham, but sent a silent wish for luck after the fleeing lovers. It was with great surprise, therefore, that he perceived a familiar travelling coach ahead of him a few minutes later. As the distance between them narrowed, he saw that it was unmistakably the one Sir George had brought to Huntington Park.

Forrest considered passing it by without stopping, but his curiosity got the better of him. He shouted to the coachman to stop as he drew his landau even with it. The startled driver pulled up the horses without protest, and a moment later Sir George himself emerged from the carriage.

"You fool, why did you stop?" he shouted to the coachman, then turned to face Forrest before he could answer.

"Very well, Dearborn, you've caught us. What is it to be, pistols at dawn?" Even in the moonlight he looked pale, but he squared his shoulders and eyed his opponent without flinching.

Forrest had to smile in spite of himself. "You have more steel in you than I had imagined, my friend," he said cheerfully. "But have you not lost your way? The turning for the North Road was nearly a mile back."

Sir George blinked, but appeared undeterred. "Don't be absurd!" he snapped. "I could not take Miss Winston-Fitts all the way to Scotland unaccompanied. She will be perfectly safe with my mother until I can obtain a Special Licence. I mailed my request to Doctor's Commons yesterday and hope to receive it within the week."

"With your mother?" echoed Forrest disbelievingly. "Then why the clandestine flight?"

"Rosalind feared that you intended to offer for her at the ball, and that her mother would force her to accept. We agreed that if we were known to have run off together, you would no longer wish to marry her, and her parents would be obliged to accept our love for each other. I intend to send word to the Winston-Fittses in the morning, to allay their natural concern for their daughter's good name."

"How very practical," Forrest had to agree. "But you are not taking Mrs. Winston-Fitts's determination to capture a title into account. I fear your plan, however sensible, will not work.''

"Pray do not attempt to stop us," said Sir George warningly. "You must see that it is me Rosalind loves." Rosalind's head appeared at the carriage window to nod vigorously.

"Oh, I have no intention of stopping you," said Forrest jovially. "I plan to help you. The only way you can be certain of thwarting Miss Winston-Fitts's ambitious mama is to head for the border."

"But...but her reputation!" Sir George and Rosalind exchanged open-mouthed glances, obviously taken aback by the earl's inexplicable attitude.

"As for that," continued Forrest, "all you need is a suitable companion for her along the way. Who better than her cousin, Miss O'Day?"

CHAPTER SEVENTEEN

ELLIE WAS WAKENED from a vivid dream, in which she and Forrest were on the verge of some understanding, by the sound of someone hammering on the front door. Blinking into the near darkness, lit only by the moon through her worn curtains, she gradually remembered where she was. As the pounding continued, she also recalled that Mrs. Flynn and a kitchen maid were the only servants in the house, and that neither was likely to answer the door at this hour. Struggling into her wrapper, she left the chamber with a yawn.

Lighting her way with a taper, Ellie made her way downstairs, still half-asleep. The knocking, which had ceased briefly, started again with renewed force as she approached the door, startling her more fully awake. In sudden alarm, she fumbled with the latch, realizing that only some dire emergency could have brought anyone here at this hour. Yanking the door open with an anxious question on her lips, she froze at the sight of the tall, familiar figure on the doorstep, certain that she must still be dreaming.

"Forrest?" she whispered doubtfully.

Looking down at Ellie as she stood before him in her thin wrapper, dark hair tumbled about her shoulders, lovely grey eyes wide with concern and confusion, Forrest was conscious of an overwhelming surge of emotion. She looked so small, so helpless, so...precious. He fought down an urge to sweep her into his arms and pour out his heart to her right then. If his kiss had frightened her into flight, there was no knowing what a sudden declaration, along with a suggestion that they immediately elope, might do! No, he must move carefully to avoid alarming her.

"Miss O'Day, I trust I find you well." Even as he spoke, Forrest was aware of the absurdity of the mundane words in such a setting. "Pray forgive me for disturbing your rest. Your cousin, Miss Winston-Fitts, has need of you."

"Rosalind? Is she ill? Hurt?" Ellie's eyes grew even wider.

"No, no," Forrest quickly reassured her. "She merely needs a chaperon—a companion."

Ellie felt as if he had dashed cold water in her face. She had no doubt now that she was fully awake. "A companion! Did Rosalind make that a condition of her marriage to you, my lord? That I be allowed to remain with her? You must be very eager indeed to wed her if you drove all this way to secure my agreement to the plan!" Ellie was fairly panting in her sudden rage. How dared he appear on her doorstep, raising her hopes again, only to make such a request?

Drawing herself up to her full height, which barely reached the earl's shoulder, Ellie said haughtily, "There are many things I would do—indeed, have already done—to ensure my cousin's happiness, Lord Dearborn, but this is not one of them. My grandfather, Lord Kerrigan, has invited me to live with him in Ireland and I mean to leave tomorrow. I am persuaded that I shall be far happier there than in the same house, or even the same country, with *you!*" She felt tears threatening and turned quickly to go, but the earl stopped her with a hand on her arm.

"I fear you have misunderstood me," he said gently to her averted face. "There is to be no marriage between Miss Winston-Fitts and myself. She needs you to play chaperon for her flight to the border with Sir George Bellamy."

Ellie turned startled eyes on him. "Her...what?" she gasped. "I am afraid I still do not understand. Rosalind and Sir George are eloping?"

"So it would seem, though they needed some persuading. Sir George, however, is concerned for his future wife's reputation should she travel to Scotland with him unaccompanied. Therefore, I suggested your services as companion to expedite matters."

"Oh!" Ellie choked on a laugh. "That...that *does* sound very like Sir George, I confess! But how do you come to be involved? Are they not running away from you as much as from my aunt and uncle?" Ellie wondered again if she could be dreaming. This whole situation seemed wildly improbable.

"There were a few awkward moments on that score, I must admit," replied Forrest cheerfully, "but I managed to convince them of my willingness to help. I don't believe Sir George realizes, even now, that the elopement was my idea in the first place."

"Your idea?" Ellie was beginning to feel almost dizzy.

"I can explain later. Will you come? I confess I will not rest easily until those two have the knot safely tied. Mrs. Winston-Fitts is a most determined woman!"

"Come? Do you mean right now?"

"Of course. Night-time is best for an elopement, don't you think? And though I don't *believe* anyone else is likely to come after them, I would as lief not take the chance. We can be well on our way to Scotland by morning."

There was much more that Ellie knew she should ask, but the thought of accompanying Forrest into the night, even with Rosalind and Sir George along, was too tempting to pass up. "I'll go and dress," she said.

"Excellent! I knew we could count on you. I shall return with the intrepid couple in a quarter of an hour," said Forrest heartily. He left the Winston-Fittses' small park in high spirits. It had cost him an effort to keep his tone light while all the time longing to crush Ellie to him, but he knew that the result would be worth it. She was coming with him to Gretna Green!

WHEN THE CARRIAGE finally stopped at an inn late the next evening, having covered more than half the distance to the border, Ellie was too tired to ask Forrest any of the questions she had rehearsed. Rosalind had slept most of the way, while the earl and Sir George took it in turns to drive the coach. She, however, had been too curious to sleep.

"Is it true?" she had asked Rosalind as soon as she saw her cousin. "Are you and Sir George really to be married?"

Rosalind nodded happily. "It was the most romantic thing, Ellie! Sir George proposed to me in the gardens yesterday and asked if I would go away with him. He explained everything so clearly . . . and when he kissed me, I felt so . . . so comfortable, so safe! I don't think I realized till that moment how much I loved him. But how do you come to be here, Ellie? I thought you back at Huntington Park with the headache!"

Ellie was momentarily at a loss for words. Her real reason for leaving seemed rather silly, given subsequent events. "I, ah, I wished to make arrangements for my trip to Ireland," she finally said. "My grandfather wrote to invite me, and even included enough money for the journey, as well as for travelling clothes. I had planned to return in time for your wedding. That is—" She broke off as it finally sank in that the wedding she had so dreaded would now never take place. "Oh, Rosie, I am so happy for you!" she suddenly cried, throwing her arms about her cousin.

Successfully diverted, Rosalind returned the embrace and then talked cheerfully of her expectations for happiness with Sir George—expectations that Ellie considered completely reasonable. She still did not understand quite how Forrest fit into the present scheme, however, and determined to find out all the details at the first opportunity.

An entire day had now passed, however, without that opportunity occurring. Forrest had slept most of the time when he had not been driving, and Rosalind's presence in the coach further inhibited Ellie from asking questions. Likewise, when they stopped for breakfast and nuncheon at posting inns along the way, there had been no chance for even a moment of private conversation with him.

In the morning, Ellie thought as she wearily followed Rosalind into the room they were to share for the night. *I shall definitely speak with him in the morning.*

IN THE MORNING, however, Ellie was the last one to awaken. By the time she was dressed and had had a bite to eat, the others were already at the carriage. Still, she made an attempt.

"My lord," she called sweetly up to Lord Dearborn as he mounted the box, "did you not promise to explain everything to me later?"

"Yes, and I certainly will, for I never break a promise," said Forrest with a grin. "If we are to reach the border by nightfall, however, we need to be off at once, miss sleepyhead!"

Ellie treated him to a withering look, but climbed into the coach without further delay.

FORREST WAS well satisfied with their progress. At their present rate of speed, they would reach Gretna Green well before dark. He was less satisfied with his handling of Ellie, however. She would not allow him to put her off much longer, he knew. The truth was, after coming so close to ruining his happiness once, he wished to be secure of her before taking any more chances. Once across the border, he could simply declare her his wife before witnesses and have no further fears of her escaping him. It was underhanded, even cowardly, he admitted, but it was also nearly foolproof.

He recalled what Ellie had said about leaving for Ireland and was doubly grateful to Sir George for his timing. If he had waited until even the next day to follow Ellie to Warwickshire, she might already have been gone! No, he would play it safe this time. Once she was wedded to him he would have ample time to court her properly. Besides, he did not think she was indifferent to him, in spite of her present—and justifiable—irritation. He chafed for the moment when he could have her all to himself, to hold her, to... He urged the horses faster.

Ellie, meanwhile, decided that in spite of the frustration of not knowing exactly what was going on, she really had little cause for complaint, considering how bleak her future had appeared only two days earlier. Rosalind was to marry Sir George rather than Lord Dearborn. She could still scarcely believe it, after so many weeks of attempting to reconcile herself to the other match, but there it was. Not only was Rosalind likely to be far happier now, but she herself was free to attempt to win the earl's heart, poor though her chances might seem. And if she were unsuccessful, which seemed likely, she still had the option of going to Ireland. Yes, either way, her future looked far rosier than it had before, when her only choice was between a loveless marriage or living indefinitely on Aunt Mabel's charity!

As the carriage rumbled northwards, Ellie began to plan how she might impress upon Forrest that he would be as happy with her as she knew she would be with him. She was not beautiful, she knew, or especially accomplished, but she and the earl appeared to have many common interests—surely that must count for something! He seemed to enjoy her company. She refused to put too much hope in that one kiss they had shared, despite the tingle that still ran through her at the memory. It might have meant nothing at all to him, she reminded herself.

Briefly, she even considered the idea of trapping him into marriage, which would be absurdly easy across the border, but quickly discarded it. No, she had to know first what his feelings for her were. If he regarded her merely as a friend, as she suspected, he would never forgive her for such a step—and that would certainly not be very conducive to a happy marriage!

Sighing, Ellie tried to settle herself for sleep. She would simply have to trust that he would make an opportunity to speak to her privately once they were in Scotland. Then she might have a chance to discover just where she stood. One thing she was determined upon: she would not leave for Ireland before she made an attempt to achieve her happiness here in England!

ALTHOUGH THE SUMMER DAYS were long, especially so far north, the sun was nearing the horizon when Forrest pulled into the yard of the first inn across the border, in the little town of Gretna Green. He had never been here before, but he felt sure there would be a blacksmith on the premises willing to marry Miss Winston-Fitts and Sir George over the anvil for a fee.

As proper as Sir George's notions were, he would surely prefer that more formal ceremony to a simple declaration before witnesses. Forrest was not so particular.

Jumping down from the box, he stretched, wondering again if he had been wise to insist on leaving Sir George's coachman behind. He opened the door to the coach and paused. All three of the occupants were soundly asleep, and his gaze lingered on Ellie where she half reclined against the far side of the coach, her head pillowed on her hand. Just as before, when he had appeared on her doorstep, he was aware of an overwhelming surge of protectiveness—a need to shield her from every danger or worry that might threaten her.

Watching Ellie as she slept peacefully, Forrest abruptly knew that he could not carry out his plan. Suppose he were mistaken about her feelings for him—he might be condemning her to a life of regret. If she would have him, he would marry her at once, but if she would not, he would try his best to forget and go on with his life. Forrest realized that he loved her too well to rob her of the choice. He could not take his own happiness at the possible expense of hers.

"Well, do you mean to sleep through your own wedding?" he asked in a loud, hearty voice, waking the sleepers. "We're here!"

Rosalind and Sir George stirred and sat up, blinking blearily. Ellie, Forrest noticed with pleasure, woke much more prettily, looking bright and refreshed, with a smile on her face.

"So this is Scotland!" she said, looking about her. "I've always wanted to visit it."

The innkeeper came out to greet them a moment later, and arrangements were quickly made for a wedding in an hour's time. Rosalind hurried inside to change into the dress she had brought along for the occasion, with Sir George solicitously at her side. Both looked excited, happy and a little frightened at what they meant to do. When Ellie would have followed Rosalind into the inn, Forrest detained her with a touch on her arm.

"I believe I promised you an explanation," he said with a smile.

"Well, it's about time!" replied Ellie, turning to him eagerly. "Now perhaps you can tell me how you came to be so intimately involved in Rosalind and Sir George's elopement. I confess, I have not been able to puzzle it out at all."

Forrest grinned down at her fondly. "Have you not? Surely you know your aunt well enough to realize that she would not relinquish a prize like myself without a struggle. As long as she was able to thrust her daughter under my nose at every opportunity I would have little chance to look elsewhere for a bride." He regarded Ellie hopefully at that point, but she was frowning.

"It was not all Aunt Mabel's fault, you know, my lord. You *did* display more than a passing interest in Rosalind. You cannot deny that."

The earl gave an exaggerated shudder. "Well I know it! My own foolishness over a pretty face nearly cost me dearly. Pray do not take offence, but I fear that your cousin would have made me a most inadequate wife.''

''Poor Rosie!'' said Ellie. ''She isn't extremely intelligent, if that is what you mean, but she does have the sweetest disposition imaginable. And she *is* beautiful.'' She regarded the earl questioningly.

''Granted,'' he said. ''But I've come to discover that I want more in a wife than mere beauty.''

As he gazed down at her with a tender enquiry in his eyes, Ellie felt the breath leave her body. ''What... what *do* you want in a wife, my lord?'' she managed to ask in a faint voice.

''I want someone who can truly share my life—its joys, its sorrows, even its absurdities. Someone I feel in tune with. I want...you, Ellie, if you will have me.''

Ellie's lips parted in wonder. ''Are...are you sure? You...you are not saying this just to be kind, are you, Forrest?'' She began to speak more quickly, before she could lose her nerve. ''I really have had a letter from my grandfather, you know, and fifty pounds besides. I can go to Ireland whenever I wish, and not be dependent on my aunt and uncle any longer. Besides, how can you possibly...?''

He silenced her with a kiss that left her no doubt about his feelings.

When they parted at last, he said, ''I feared that you might prove stubborn. I should tell you that I am fully prepared to shout before all who can hear me that you are my wife. Then you will be quite trapped.''

Ellie dissolved into giggles. ''No, would you really?'' she gasped. ''You may not believe it, but on the way here, I considered doing the same thing to you!''

Forrest stared at her for an instant, then burst out laughing. "Suppose... suppose we had done so simultaneously. Imagine..." His words were lost in laughter. They clung to each other until they had laughed themselves out, finally catching their breath and wiping the tears from their eyes.

"May I take it then, that you will do me the honour of becoming my wife, Miss O'Day?" he asked when he could speak again.

Ellie nodded silently, her eyes still dancing, afraid that if she opened her mouth she would begin laughing again. "You... you may," she managed shakily.

"Well then—" Forrest was suddenly brisk "—we had best speak to the innkeeper at once to see if we can make this a double wedding." He took Ellie's hand and she accompanied him into the inn, her heart light as a feather.

CHAPTER EIGHTEEN

IT WAS a very contented quartet that headed south late the next morning. Forrest and Sir George had decided to hire a coachman for the return trip, so that both of them could spend the entire journey inside with their new brides. Ellie and Rosalind were radiant, each revelling in the other's happiness nearly as much as in her own.

During the first day's drive, Forrest explained how he had prompted Sir George to elope with the story of his fictitious friend and all of them enjoyed a good laugh over it, though Rosalind never seemed to get it all quite straight. For her part, Rosalind declared that she had known from the first that Forrest and Ellie were perfect for each other.

"I knew you cared for her a month ago, my lord," she informed him. "Why, when we danced at Almack's you could speak of no one but Ellie, do you not recall?" Proudly, she recounted her matchmaking attempts on their behalf, earning chuckles and no small amount of respect for her foresight, all the more remarkable for its singularity.

With this and other reminiscences of the Season past, the four enjoyed a merry journey. Not until noon on the third day from Gretna Green, as they were once more nearing Huntington Park, did the mood in the carriage become a trifle less jolly.

"I say, Dearborn," said Sir George as the gates came within sight, "I'm deuced glad that you'll be with me when I face Mrs. Winston-Fitts with the news. What do you say we make our announcement as publicly as possible?" He seemed to have lost much of his stodginess over the past three days.

"An excellent idea," agreed Forrest. "That might save us from the worst of her initial reaction. I fear, Miss, er, Lady Bellamy, that your mother will be less than overjoyed at the results of our little jaunt."

Rosalind dimpled prettily. "She will simply have to grow accustomed to it, my lord. Surely, once she sees how happy I am, and how happy Ellie is, she can have no objections."

"Ever the optimist, Rosie," said Ellie wryly. "For myself, I'd as soon be out of the way when Aunt Mabel first hears how things have fallen out." Happiness had overshadowed any such fears during their journey, but now she was aware of a growing nervousness. Forrest apparently sensed it, for he gave her hand an encouraging squeeze.

"Come now," he said bracingly as the carriage turned up the drive. "What is the worst she can do? She will no longer have the authority to send you to your room, you know—which, by the by, will be my chamber now." He waggled his brows suggestively at her, causing her to giggle.

"If she does, I shall obey her with alacrity, my lord," she told her husband with a bewitching smile.

"I HEAR A CARRIAGE, I am certain of it!" cried Mrs. Winston-Fitts, hurrying to the parlour window for the tenth time that morning. She had been so fidgety for the past five days as to drive everyone else distracted.

Lady Dearborn devoutly hoped that whoever was approaching brought some word of the runaway lovers—preferably that they were now in Warwickshire, awaiting the Winston-Fittses there! She was sick to death of the whole business, though she wondered that Forrest and Miss O'Day had not yet returned. His eagerness to be off had convinced her that his goal had nothing to do with the eloping couple.

Most likely, she thought, he had decided to wait in Warwickshire until Sir George and his new bride could reasonably be expected back, in order to spare Miss O'Day the worst of her aunt's wrath. The woman had given ample demonstration over the past few days just how unpleasant she could be when crossed. Lady Dearborn could not blame those of her guests—all but Lady Emma and her daughter and, of course, the Glenhavens—who had decided to make an early departure. Even her assurance that she would instantly send along any news she received to Warwickshire had not succeeded in ridding her of the Winston-Fittses, however. It was plain that the woman had not yet given up hope of seeing her daughter the next Countess of Dearborn.

"Oh, oh! There is my Rosalind! Lord Dearborn has brought her back!" Mrs. Winston-Fitts exclaimed at that moment from her post at the window. "I knew he would manage it! Sir George is here, as well. Emmett, I know duelling is illegal, but perhaps you can have him taken up for abduction or some such thing. Such presumption! I wonder that Lord Dearborn did not call him out! And there is Elinor, too—how strange! I suppose Lord Dearborn fetched her to act as chaperon for Rosalind. He must care for her very much to have thought of it! But, la! Five days! Why, they must have been nearly to the border before—''

Lady Dearborn waited to hear no more. At first mention of her son, she was halfway to the parlour door, her puce shawl trailing forgotten behind her, to the delight of Charm and Token, who had once again sought out their mistress. Hutchins had already opened the front door when she reached it.

''Forrest!'' she cried from the top step, attracting the attention of the four young people below her, who were clustered together in whispered conversation. The rest of the house guests crowded behind her in the doorway.

''Good afternoon, Mother,'' responded the earl jovially, doffing his hat and sweeping the gathered company an elegant bow. ''I hope we have not worried you unduly.''

Mrs. Winston-Fitts, having delayed at the window, came up last and pushed her way through the interested onlookers. ''Worried! Indeed we have been, my lord,'' she declared before anyone else could speak. ''I am more grateful than I can express that you have brought my daughter back. Oh, my precious!'' Rushing forward, she clasped Rosalind to her. ''Whatever could you have been thinking of to use me so! I was nigh out of my mind with anxiety!''

"I am sorry we worried you, Mama, but I am persuaded it was for the best," said Rosalind, with commendable bravery. "I hope you will wish me happy as Sir George's wife."

"Wife! Wife? You are actually married! Then you were not in time to stop them, my lord? Oh, but surely we can have it annulled! Rosalind is but eighteen!" Ashen-faced, she looked from Rosalind to Sir George, who had draped a possessive arm about her shoulders.

"I think not, ma'am," he said placidly. "The ceremony was duly witnessed and perfectly legal. Lady Bellamy and I are in great hopes that you will come to regard our match with as much joy as we do."

Mrs. Winston-Fitts opened and closed her mouth several times, plainly at a loss. Seeking an outlet for her frustration, she turned suddenly on her niece. "You, miss! I suppose you knew of this all along and ran off to Warwickshire to avoid telling me! I shall have to devise a suitable punishment for such perfidy."

Ellie was unmoved by her aunt's threat. In fact, recalling what Forrest had said earlier on that score, she felt the corners of her mouth begin to twitch. Mrs. Winston-Fitts noticed at once.

"Do you dare laugh in my face?" she fairly shrieked. "You ungrateful hussy! After all I have done for you!" She raised her hand as though to slap Ellie's face, but the earl quickly interposed himself between them.

"I will thank you, madam, to refrain from insulting my wife," he said in a chilly voice.

His words brought her up short. "Your...what did you say, my lord?"

"Your niece has done me the honour of becoming my wife," he repeated. "Ma'am, may I present the new Countess of Dearborn?" he asked, turning to his mother, who had by that time come up to stand next to him. "You did always say you longed to become a dowager, did you not?"

Lady Dearborn broke into a delighted smile. "Indeed I did, Forrest. Welcome, my dear. I could not be happier." She embraced Ellie warmly.

The rest of the company, as though freed from a spell by the new dowager countess's action, surged round the two newly married couples, offering good wishes and congratulations.

"Oh, Ellie, I am so happy for both of you!" exclaimed Juliet, hugging her new sister. "I prayed that it might turn out so!"

Mr. Winston-Fitts stepped forward to shake Sir George's hand. "Well done, my boy!" he said jovially. "I can think of no one who could make my daughter happier." He bent a commanding look on his wife and, after a few deep breaths, Mrs. Winston-Fitts managed to summon up a sickly smile.

"At least you will not be removing very far from me, Rosalind," she said, giving her daughter a kiss on the cheek. "You have captured a treasure, Sir George," she said severely to her new son-in-law. "See that you treat her as such."

Slowly, they all moved into the house. Everyone was talking and laughing at once, asking questions and giving animated replies. As soon as they entered the parlour, Forrest rang for punch all round to celebrate, while his mother bade the footman bring in a tray of Cook's best pastries. In the midst of all this hilarity, Hutchins delivered the afternoon post to Lord Dearborn on a tray.

"Here, Mother," he said, handing the stack of letters to her. "I do not doubt most of this is for you. Put any business letters aside for me to deal with later. I could not do them justice at the moment."

Lady Dearborn glanced quickly through the papers, impatient to continue her talk with her new daughter-in-law, pausing to open only one letter.

"My goodness!" she exclaimed as she read it through. "It is from Lord Kerrigan, your grandfather, my dear. He is quite recovered, it seems, and was delighted to learn that I had made your acquaintance. He expresses a desire to see me again and asks if I would consider escorting you to Ireland. For the sake of old friendship, of course!"

Ellie noticed that the dowager's cheeks had pinkened somewhat. "I must tell him of my marriage at once, of course," she said. "'Twould be wonderful if I could do so in person." She looked questioningly to her husband as she spoke.

"A splendid notion, I think," said Forrest at once. "In fact, I had already thought that Ireland might be just the place to begin our wedding trip. My mother may remain there when we continue on to the Continent, if she wishes." The look he directed at the dowager countess was one of mingled amusement and curiosity.

The dowager's blush deepened, but she said composedly enough, "Perhaps I shall. No one I know can play whist as Kerrigan used to. The four of us will have some rare games, I doubt not."

"Pray do not expect Ellie and me to spend an inordinate time at the card table," said Forrest with a wink at his new countess. "We shall have other things to occupy our time."

The dowager snorted, and began to make plans for the trip. "Let me see, if we wait another week 'twill be after the new moon, the best possible time to set out." She stopped with a gasp. "Forrest! Do you realize you were married on a waning moon? Of course, had you waited it would no longer be June, and that is the luckiest month for weddings—"

"Mother," interrupted the earl in a commanding tone, "you will please to keep your superstitions to yourself. I attempted to follow the advice of your Madame Fortunata, and look where it almost led me."

"She was nearly right, you know, Forrest," she protested. "I must confess that the description of your bride was my idea, and sadly mistaken." She smiled fondly at Ellie and reached out to squeeze her hand. "But she did predict your marriage this year. The stars are never wrong!"

Forrest looked deep into Ellie's eyes. "Whether luck or the stars had anything to do with it or not, I am eternally grateful that I finally found my soul mate," he said. In front of the entire company, he bestowed a tender, lingering kiss on Elinor, the Countess of Dearborn—his Destiny.

Harlequin is proud to present our best authors, their best books and the best for your reading pleasure!

Throughout 1993, Harlequin will bring you exciting books by some of the top names in contemporary romance!

In February, look for *Twist of Fate* by

Hannah Jessett had been content with her quiet life. Suddenly she was the center of a corporate battle with wealthy entrepreneur Gideon Cage. Now Hannah must choose between the fame and money an inheritance has brought or a love that may not be as it appears.

Don't miss TWIST OF FATE ...
wherever Harlequin books are sold.

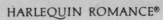

Where do you find hot Texas nights, smooth Texas charm and dangerously sexy cowboys?

DEEP IN THE HEART

Wedding Bells—Texas Style!

Even a Boston blue blood needs a Texas education. Ranch owner J. T. McKinney is handsome, strong, opinionated and totally charming. And he is determined to marry beautiful Bostonian Cynthia Page. However, the couple soon discovers a Texas cattleman's idea of marriage differs greatly from a New England career woman's!

CRYSTAL CREEK reverberates with the exciting rhythm of Texas. Each story features the rugged individuals who live and love in the Lone Star State. And each one ends with the same invitation...

Y'ALL COME BACK...REAL SOON!

Don't miss *DEEP IN THE HEART* by Barbara Kaye. Available in March wherever Harlequin books are sold.

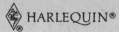

HARLEQUIN®

my Valentine

1993

The most romantic day of the year is here! Escape into the exquisite world of love with MY VALENTINE 1993. What better way to celebrate Valentine's Day than with this very romantic, sensuous collection of four original short stories, written by some of Harlequin's most popular authors.

ANNE STUART
JUDITH ARNOLD
ANNE McALLISTER
LINDA RANDALL WISDOM

THIS VALENTINE'S DAY, DISCOVER ROMANCE
WITH MY VALENTINE 1993

Available in February wherever Harlequin Books are sold.　　VAL93